Silver Myths and Legends of the World

Geraldine McCaughrean was born in North London. Her degree was in Education and she has been writing full time for many years, both adult and children's books. She has won the Whitbread Award, the Guardian Children's Fiction Award, the Carnegie Medal and the Beefeater Children's Book Award and has written several books for Orion, including *Myths and Legends of the World: The Golden Hoard, The Silver Treasure, The Bronze Cauldron* and *The Crystal Pool, Cowboy Jess* and *Cowboy Jess Saddles Up*. She lives in Berkshire with her husband John and daughter Ailsa.

Other books by the same author

Myths and Legends of the World: *The Golden Hoard*
Myths and Legends of the World: *The Silver Treasure*
Myths and Legends of the World: *The Bronze Cauldron*
Myths and Legends of the World: *The Crystal Pool*
Cowboy Jess
Cowboy Jess Saddles Up

Silver Myths and Legends of the World

Geraldine McCaughrean

A Dolphin
Paperback

First published in Great Britain in 1999
by Orion Children's Books
a division of the Orion Publishing Group Ltd
Orion House
5 Upper St Martin's Lane
London WC2H 9EA

A catalogue record for this book is available
from the British Library

Typeset at The Spartan Press Ltd
Lymington, Hants
Printed in Great Britain by
Clays Ltd, St Ives plc

ISBN 1 85881 676 9

Contents

The Silver-Miners

A LEGEND FROM BOLIVIA

WHEN THE Spanish came to South America, they looked round them at the people, but saw only the gold bands on their arms, the silver rings in their ears. They looked at the great stepped temples, like stairways to Heaven, and saw no gods but only the golden chalices and silver plates the priests held. When they looked at Bolivia, beautiful with holy green mountains, they saw only huge heaps of earth threaded with silver ore. They saw no beauty but in digging, gouging, tearing. They sank silver mines.

Worse. They did not even do the digging themselves, but forced the local people into a slavery of breaking and carrying rocks. The mountain Parichata, husband mountain of Tata-Turqui, guardian of Potosí Town, was torn and pounded with picks and shovels, and his silver ripped out to feed Spanish greed.

'O Parichata, forgive us!' groaned the labourers, swinging their long picks as the midday sun scorched down on them. 'O Parichata, grieve with us!' they sobbed as they staggered beneath huge baskets of rock. 'O Parichata, husband of Tata-Turqui, guardian of Potosí Town, have pity on us! Would that you were made all of mud and had not a grain of silver in you, that you might stand at peace in the landscape, and we beside you!'

But the air was so full of the sound of whips that their prayers seemed to be cracked and broken by the lash in mid-air, and to fall to the ground without ever reaching the ears of the gods. Only the crawling beetles on the ground waved their long antennae and scuttled away.

Each evening, at the end of the day's work, Maro the mule-boy would lead his father's skinny mules up the mountain path to the mines. It was his job to ensure the animals were ready and waiting for the first loads of the following day. The Spaniards paid Maro's father nothing, and the animals were already half-dead with overwork. 'But better they should drop in their tracks,' his father said, 'than that mothers and children should die carrying rocks for these slave-drivers.'

Suddenly, Maro heard ahead of him on the path the clatter of hooves. More donkeys? How very strange. He had thought his was the only team for miles around. And when the mules appeared, they quite took his breath away, for not only were they glossy, sleek and fat, but coal-black in coat and mane. Huge panniers were strapped to both sides of their saddles.

The muleteer driving them wore a straw hat which cast his face into shadow despite a bright moon. 'Out of the way, boy!' he shouted at Maro. 'Clear the path! Go back or die!'

'I shall die if I don't do as the Spaniards tell me,' said Maro, but the muleteer uttered such a fearsome roar that both Maro and his donkeys scampered off the path in terror, and the black mules clattered on downwards, unhindered. Maro ran after all his animals, gathered up their lead-ropes and led them back down to the edge of town.

But his curiosity got the better of him. He could not bear not to know what was happening to his beloved mountain, and going back alone, on silent, bare feet, he hid himself beside the path and watched all night.

He saw, under the moonlight, how the chalky path was alive with insect-life. Whole swarms of gleaming longicorn beetles, bugs and mud-rollers were crawling upwards.

Every beetle on Parichata seemed to be closing in on the silver mines.

Rank by rank, the beetles reached the mine workings – where the trees were all felled, the boulders smashed, the flowers uprooted and the mountain's flesh cut to its very bones of silver. There, the Indian in the straw hat was waiting. He touched each beetle with his muleteer's goad, and rolled it on to its glossy back.

But when they rolled back again on to their feet, the feet they stood on were hooves, the legs they straightened were hairy, and their bodies and heads were those of fully grown handsome mules. In place of their antennae were long pink-lined ears, and over their backs the muleteer hung panniers of woven wicker-work.

Out of the mountain flowed molten silver. It spouted and spurted in fountains and springs, directly into the panniers, and there solidified into shining ingots. With both panniers full, each mule turned down the mountain path and came clumping past Maro's hiding place before disappearing into the black distance, leaving only the echo of hooves clip-clopping among the rocks.

The Spaniards arrived next morning, eager and anxious for a new day's loot. Their wary slaves rolled miserably out of bed and crawled up the pocked and scarred mountainside. They found (to their amazement) that there was no silver to mine.

The Spaniards looked – oh, how they looked! – sinking new drill holes, scrambling down every crevice, peeling back the grass as though they would flay the mountain. But they could find no trace of silver, not the merest grain, not the tiniest glitter. It was as if Parichata had been filleted of all his silver bones.

'You won't find any.' Maro spoke up from between the muzzles of his father's mules. His neighbours looked round at him in astonishment. The Spaniards scowled. 'Parichata took pity on us last night. He gave away his silver for the sake of the people.' And Maro went on to tell them how every beetle had been turned into a mule and had carried away the precious ore. The Spanish only snorted with disbelief, but the people of Potosí Town looked down at the ground, and saw no beetles, no, not so much as a leather beetle creeping to and fro.

No one ever discovered where the beetle-mules took their treasure of silver. Perhaps they gave it into the safe keeping of Tata-Turqui, wife-mountain of Parichata, or perhaps they carried it into the valleys, to some secret treasure-house. But though the Spaniards raged and threatened, they had, in the end, to quit Potosí and seek their riches elsewhere.

The scars on the face of Parichata soon healed. Spring brought its yearly treasure of seeds, berries, flowers and sapling trees. And after morning had dropped its dew on every spider's web and leaf and bending blade of grass, Parichata was not entirely without a gleam of silver in the early dawn.

The Men in the Moon

A MYTH FROM KENYA

'**M**URILAY, come here! Murilay, don't do that! Murilay, I've told you before! Murilay, just wait till your father comes home!'

Murilay hunched his shoulders and slunk out of doors. He could hear his mother's shrill voice still scolding inside the hut, her words hunting after him like stinging red ants.

A wooden stool stood beside the door – the carved seat where Murilay's father liked to sit in the evenings and watch the huge sun shimmer and ripple, and the clean sharp-edged rising Moon cut its way like a sickle through the last stems of cloud, the stars raining. 'We may have nothing,' Murilay's father liked to say, pointing at the sky with his knurled and gnarled old walking stick, 'but we are as rich in stars as the next man.'

Murilay liked to watch the sunset, too, but his mother never let him sit down for long enough. 'Eat your supper, Murilay! Wash your face, Murilay! Go to bed, Murilay, and get up a better boy. The boys in the Moon never cheek their mother. The boys in the Moon always do as they're told. The boys in the Moon aren't lazy, idle, good-for-nothing boys like you!'

Murilay seized his chance to sit, for once, upon his father's stool. 'The boys in the Moon are lucky,' he said out loud. 'I wish I could be up there in the peace and quiet.'

The stool rocked, the stool swayed, the stool reared up like a horse, and it was all Murilay could do not to tumble off. The stool took a practice leap into the branches of a nearby tree, and balanced there, quivering with pent-up magic.

Murilay was excited. 'Up, stool, up!' he said. 'Up to the Moon!'

The stool rose further up, resting at intervals on a cloudbank, a ledge of rainbow. Finally, the blue sky gave way to the blackness of space, and Murilay flew on his stool as far as the Moon, where he landed in a pleasant landscape yellow with Moon-bleached grass.

A group of men came by driving cows ahead of them. They cast a wary eye over the boy sitting on a stool in the middle of nowhere.

'Please, gentlemen,' Murilay asked politely, 'can you direct me to the Chief of the Moon People?'

They knew at once he was a stranger, and grinned in a way not entirely friendly. 'You want directions? You earn them. You work for us for a month.'

So Murilay worked for the men, grooming their cows and fetching water from the deep wells of the Moon. His mother's nagging had accustomed Murilay to worse than anything these men could inflict, and he was not unhappy. Time only hung heavy because the food was so *bad*. At the end of each day the cowherds gave him stone-cold porridge, uncooked and indigestible. He might have understood, if they had eaten differently – but they ate the same themselves!

'I have worked one month for you. Now tell me, gentlemen, where I may find the Chief of the Moon People.' The cowherds gave a variety of grunts and pointed out a path. Murilay ran down it before they could change their minds.

The path did indeed bring him to the village of the Moon Chief. It was a dark, dismal place, and very cold. The people huddled under blankets in the doorways of their huts, crunching nuts between broken teeth, or sipping cold porridge. The Chief himself sat on a carved wooden chair watching the Earth rise, like a green-and-blue duck egg, alongside a sprinkling of stars. The first remark he made to Murilay was, 'We may not have much to call our own, stranger, but we are as rich in stars as the next village.' He waved in one fist a giant turkey wing still stubbly from plucking and completely raw.

When he offered Murilay something to eat, a servant brought the meat of a Moon rabbit; that, too, dripped blood.

'Eat, eat, young man! Don't stand on ceremony! You must be very hungry if you've travelled all the way from Earth and done a month's work as well!'

'The gods forbid that I should offend your highness,' said Murilay, 'and I realize that the fault is all mine, but I am accustomed to eating my food . . . how can I say this? . . . cooked.'

'Cooked? How "cooked"? What does it mean?' said the Chief, scowling over his turkey wing.

'With fire,' said Murilay.

'Fire? And what's that?'

The Chief's wives were glaring at Murilay from under the blankets, dark eyes enveloped in wool and temper. Murilay began to see the Moon in quite a new light. He searched about for two flints, pulled a tuft of hair from his head for kindling and – to the great astonishment of the whole tribe – struck a spark.

He fanned it to a flame, fed it with wood and, looking about for food to cook, took the turkey drumstick from the Chief's hand. Warrior bodyguards lifted their spears menacingly. But Murilay persevered in cooking the turkey on the fire, while the People of the Moon were busy discovering the delights of warmth. They crept from under their blankets. They gazed round-eyed at the leaping fire, and burnt themselves trying to pick it up.

'To think that my mother thought these folk were far

above us!' thought Murilay, but kept the thought to himself.

When the Chief of the Moon tasted his roast turkey, he at once offered Murilay all his daughters as wives.

Murilay had not been planning to marry so young, but the prospect of marrying seven princesses in one day quite changed his outlook. Gifts of cattle and sheep followed the marriage, and by nightfall, Murilay was proclaimed the greatest magician in the Realm of Stars.

While Murilay grew to manhood, the People of the Moon prospered as they had never done before. By the time he had a hut and a family of children, his wealth was second only to the Chief's.

But sometimes, when he sat on his father's wooden stool and watched the Earth rising, he longed to see, from Earth, the Moon cut cleanly through the last stems of evening cloud. He wanted to see his father again and hear the crows in the treetops at dusk, as shrill as his darling mother.

He decided to go back, but going was not as simple as coming. He might fly back on his magic stool, as easily as the birds hopped between Earth and Moon, but he had his wives and cows and children and sheep to think of. All on one stool, they would find the journey hugely over-crowded. There was a place where the Moon dipped down and the Earth sloped up, and a causeway joined the two. But it would be a difficult, dangerous journey to make. So he sent word ahead, by way of the Mockingbird, telling his family to meet him halfway and help with the cattle.

'Muri-i-i-lay! Muri-i-i-lay! Home soon, home soon!' squawked the Mockingbird, and gave a burst of brash, brittle laughter. 'Meet him halfway to the Moon!'

Murilay's father picked up a stone and threw it. 'Wicked bird! Do you want to break my heart with your lies? My Murilay is dead these seven years!'

'Muri-i-i-lay be home soon!' cackled the bird. But

Murilay's mother came after it with a broom, and cursed it with a dozen curses for lying about her poor dead son. The Mockingbird flew back to the Moon and explained the problem to Murilay.

'You lazy, idle, good-for-nothing, laze-in-the-sun-all-day, lying bird!' exclaimed Murilay. 'You never even went there! My parents would never give me up for dead, just because I disappeared for a few years!'

The poor Mockingbird flew back down to Earth and swooped low over the house of Murilay's parents. It snatched the knurled and gnarled walking stick out of the old man's hand. The old man stood up, but the bird flew out of reach of his old, weak hands. He watched until the bird flew out of sight of his old, weak eyes.

Then Murilay had to accept that he must make the journey all by himself, and set off for Earth with his wives and children and cattle and sheep, skidding down the slopes of Moon-white scree.

The cattle slid on their hocks, Murilay skidded on his heels, the white Moon-dust filling his hair and clogging his throat. A trail of milk, white as Moonlight, dripped from the udders of the cows. Murilay's wives and children soon grew tired and rode on the backs of the cows.

Then Murilay grew weary, too, and feared he could go no further. When he reached the causeway joining the Moon to the Earth, he sat down with his head between his knees and wept. For the causeway passed over a bottomless chasm so terrifying that Murilay dared not go one step across it. He was already dizzy with weariness, and his courage was fading fast.

'I will carry you across.'

'Who said that?'

'I did,' said the Bull. 'I'll carry you over, if you promise my reward won't be the butcher's knife. I've seen what your fire does to meat, and I daresay beef is dear to you People of Earth.'

'I promise I shall never eat red meat, if you will carry me over the Ravine of Nothingness,' vowed Murilay.

So the Bull took Murilay on its back and, as sure-footed as any mountain goat, tripped across the knife-edge narrow isthmus to the great meadows of Africa.

That evening, Murilay's father and mother sat on the ground outside their hut. (The stool was gone which had once stood there.) They watched the sun set – saw its big mottled face dip beneath the fumes of dusk and waver like the thinnest wafer of gold leaf. Then the Moon rose, clean and sharp-edged as a scythe, and cut its way through the last stems of evening cloud. The stars rained.

'I would give every star in the sky to see my son again,' said the old man to his wife, and his wife said, 'So would I.'

Out of the darkness came the lowing of a hundred cattle, and off the plain came a herd of Moon-white cows led by a coppery bull. Riding on the Bull was Murilay, their long-lost son, as rich as the richest, as fit as the fittest, as happy as the happiest, pointing at the stars with a knurled and gnarled stick and singing a song he had learned on the Moon.

Dream Journey

A MAORI MYTH

THERE was once a great chieftain, whose mind was as wide as the plain, and whose dreams were as bright as sunshine. One night, a dream shone on his sleep that was almost too dazzling to comprehend, but it filled him with feelings of great hope and excitement. 'Go north,' said the voice in his dream. 'Go north, and I will show you the shape of happiness.'

> *Go alone, without a sound,*
> *Like the shadow of a bird*
> *Passing over broken ground,*
> *Or flies' flicker. Be not heard*
> *More than time passing.'*

Kahakura was so thrilled by his dream that he got up at once and ran down to the beach to tell his people. The young men of his tribe stood about, balanced precariously on the seaside rocks, aiming spears at the fish in the water. They would throw, jump in, retrieve their spears and begin again. Their catch lay on the shore – a couple of bass and a flatfish.

'I must go away! I've dreamed a dream,' announced Kahakura. 'I've seen a vision. I've been made a promise by the gods! Stay here and wait: I'm going north to fetch the gift the gods have promised us!'

The young men stood on one leg and stared at him open-mouthed. Go away? Leave them without a chief and go north into hostile country? Not if they could help it.

'We'll come with you!' they said, jumping down into the surf. 'We'll all go!' They wanted neither to miss out on the adventure nor to see their chief disappear over the horizon without knowing when or if he would return. So although Kahakura insisted he must go alone, they dogged his footsteps round the settlement and stuck as fast to him as his own shadow. Kahakura began to think he might not be able to do as his dream instructed: his own people would stop him making whatever marvellous discovery awaited him in the north.

One evening, when the whole village was dancing, the music loud and the singing cacophonous, Kahakura backed away into the surrounding darkness. He cast a last fond look at his people dancing in a pool of firelight, then turned and began to run – northwards.

For many days, he trekked through the provinces of tribes whose warriors would have speared him as eagerly as fishermen spearing a fish. But Kahakura wove his way through the grey tassels at either end of day, when the ground is carpeted neither with light nor dark.

At long last, he came to a country called Rangiaowhia, fluffy with white flax and fringed with yellow sand. He first glimpsed the sea in the early morning. It seemed to Kahakura that the moon, in leaving the sky, must have fallen and smashed. For the sea was silver with sparkling lozenges of metallic light. Then the water began to rattle and leap, to explode with fish, such crowds of them that they shouldered each other out of the water to somersault in the surf. A feast of fish! Kahakura's first instinct was to race into the surf and gather them up in armfuls – but instead, he hid himself. He was not first on the scene. Someone was already busy catching the fish.

The fishermen were the frail, slender, tiny Sea People – a tribe who live among the ocean waves and come ashore only as often as the Land people put out to sea. Kahakura had heard tell of them, and now here they were – in front of his very eyes – fishing. And not with spears!

Looking once more at the multitude of fish in the bay, Kahakura saw that they were being hauled in and harvested in a giant bag – a spider's web of woven thread, delicate as hair, yet strong as sinew. When the mouth of the bag was closed, inside it were trapped not one fish or two, but one or two *thousand*!

Kahakura stared. '*This* is what I was sent here to see,' he thought. 'A way of catching fish which will feed my tribe for all time! As long as the sea runs and fish run in the sea, we'll never be hungry again! I must take that bag home with me, to copy how it is made.'

From his hiding place, Kahakura watched the Sea People struggle. Though they were pretty with their yellow hair and pale, smooth skins, they were a puny race, narrow-chested, thin-shanked, with pinched moonish faces. It took twenty men to land the catch, whereas Kahakura could have done it with a couple of friends.

The work done, the young men lay about exhausted among their canoes, while their blond-haired women gutted and cleaned the fish. A flock of gulls gathered to eat the offal, and frightened the Sea People's tiny children.

Apart from the other women sat a girl quite different from the rest. She had the task of mending the net. Children sat about her feet, laughing at the stories and jokes she told them, but the other women sat with their backs turned, and threw her not so much as a civil word. Perhaps it was her beauty which made them resent her. Perhaps it was her formidable size which made the men equally unkind. Taller than the tallest fishermen, she had hips like the curving bole of a tree, and arms strong enough to carry a family of children. Her clever hands wove and knotted flaxen thread into the holes where the net had torn. Kahakura was so entranced by the sight of her and her quick, darting fingers that he almost forgot why the gods had sent him to Rangiaowhia.

The net!

He jumped up from his hiding place, thinking to tell the Sea People . . . what? As his head rose above the bushes, he realized he had not even thought what to say, or how to come by the precious net which now lay stretched at the girl's feet. He had nothing to trade for it, no weapon to fight for it, and the language of the Sea People was strange to him. So when they caught sight of him, he spoke with a great loud voice – as people do to make foreigners understand them.

'I am Kahakura of the Maori People! I dreamed a dream and I saw a vision . . . Wait, don't go!'

The Sea People took one look at his towering frame, huge shoulders, broad chest. Then mothers snatched up their children and threw them into the canoes, jumping in after them. The men plunged into the surf and dragged the canoes out to sea.

The big yellow-haired girl took two steps from her seat and fell, her feet tangled in the net she had been mending. Her basket of threads and tools was squandered on the ground. For a moment, Kahakura thought to bundle her up in the net like a giant tuna, and sling her over his back. He had to have her for his wife, stroke that golden hair, and watch her bounce his children on her knee.

But the thought came to him – as clearly as the dream had come to him in sleeping – that a man does not take a wife in the same way as a fisherman takes a tuna. So he stood just where he was, and allowed her to untangle her feet and get up.

She ran a few steps towards the sea – saw her tribe and family paddling away from her, abandoning her, but did not cry out. She looked back to where Kahakura stood wearing a crooked, uncertain smile. He gathered up the spilled tools and thread and handed the basket back to her.

'It is as the gods wish, or my eyes would not have seen you,' he said. And she seemed to understand.

So Kahakura took home to his tribe the amazing secret of fishing nets – how they are used and how they are made. And he took home, too, a wife with golden hair, and curved hips like the bole of a flourishing tree, and strong arms destined to hold a family of children. As long as the sea runs, and the fish run in the sea, the Maori People will never go hungry for fish, nor empty of love. It is as the gods wish.

Roland and the Horn Olivant

A LEGEND FROM FRANCE

THE KNIGHTS of Charlemagne were like the spring flowers which brighten fields as far as the eye can see. Resplendent with flapping pennons and banners of purple silk, the army prinked its way on high-prancing horses over the faces of the fallen enemy; its minstrels outsang the evening birds. Saddlecloths swept the ground like the skirts of the women waiting at home for the knights of Charlemagne, the finest men in all the world. And finest of them all was Roland.

Even in retreat they were magnificent. They carried their wounds like the red rosettes of victory, and they died with a joke and a prayer. The army of Charlemagne was like the spring which covers the fields in flowers . . . but the Saracens were like the locusts which strip fields bare. Though the Emperor Charlemagne had conquered most of the world, the Saracens denied him the realms of Spain. Their troops massed to turn him back, as tightly packed as bricks in a wall. In the end, there was no more purpose to be served in throwing good men against such a wall to seem them break, and Charlemagne withdrew. His knights were the finest in all the world, and the finest of them all was Roland.

'Sir Roland, my friend and pride of my knights,' said Charlemagne, 'command the rearguard, I beg you, and shelter the wounded and the weary from attack as we retreat.'

'I shall, my lord – if we really must leave Spain unconquered.'

'Better to withdraw and come back another day, eh, than grant the enemy our blood to walk in and our shields to decorate their halls . . .? Do you have Olivant with you?'

Sir Roland nodded and pointed to his horse. Hung by a scarlet cord from his saddle was a huge horn – the tusk of an elephant, carved by Roland's own hand, reamed and bored with fire and hot steel. No one but Roland could blow it, and there was no sound like the shriek of Horn Olivant. 'If you need reinforcements,' said the Emperor, 'sound Olivant, and I shall turn back to help you.'

Roland, in his pride, bridled a little, and his cheeks flushed. 'I shall summon you, my lord, if I prove unequal to my task.'

The army began to move. Like a frozen river thawed by spring, it moved between the craggy mountain passes. First came Charlemagne with his princes, dukes and earls, then his knights, squires and foot-soldiers; next the wagons and the wagonboys, the armourers, farriers and fletchers; the machinery and engines of war. After, came the dead, fetched out of battle by their friends for decent burial in a Christian land; and behind them, moving with painful slowness, came the wounded and the sick, wearing blood-stained banners for blankets, and marching in silence, without breath enough for song.

Behind them came the troops of Roland, half-turned in their saddles to watch for pursuers.

'Charlemagne leaving Spain? By the God I serve, he shall not!' declared the great Sultan in his marble courts. 'Pursue him with sword and arrow and let not one man live who has offended me by setting foot in Spain! No, when your work is done let not two letters of that filthy name hang together: *Charlemagne*!'

At Roncesvalles it happened. The Saracens came down like wolves upon a flock of sheep. When Roland saw the dust raised by their horses' hooves, he wheeled his knights about and deployed them as a blockade across the path, to shield the column of retreating Franks. Roland made a wall of men to stop the Saracen rout.

'We shall be the reef on which they founder!' he shouted to his men, and the sight of his great war horse, prancing from end to end of the human wall, put heart into his battalion and fired them with resolve. 'Ours is the honour of saving Charlemagne's army, that he may go on to win new victories! Ours is the honour of doing our duty! Let us leave the Saracens with one last taste of our mettle! Let's write one last page of history!'

And it seemed as though that page would be written in gold. For five tides of Saracens broke against the reef of Frankish Knights, but it held fast, and they could not break through. Like summer flies the Saracens fell, while the Frankish shields held firm, edge to edge – a palisade painted with heraldic beasts. At long last, the Saracens withdrew and the weary knights drew breath and congratulated one another on their daring and skill.

Then five more battalions of Saracens appeared over the rocky horizon.

So the page of history was to be written in blood, after all. As the five tides broke against the Frankish reef, soldiers too weary any longer to lift a sword were trampled down. Knights wounded in the first onslaught found their limbs too cold to raise lance or axe, and fell beneath Saracen swords. When, at last, the tenth battalion was driven off, the splendour of Charlemagne's rearguard was as tattered as a windfrayed banner. Still, the wall had held. The column of wounded and sick crept away around distant bends in the mountain track.

'The day is ours and all the honour!' cried Roland exultantly. 'I did not sound the Horn Olivant, for we alone did what was asked of us!' He rose proudly in his stirrups.

. . . That was when he glimpsed the dust of five battalions more.

'Sound the horn now, my lord!' exclaimed his sergeant. 'Signal the Emperor that we are outnumbered!'

'And lose the honour of the day? Plead for help, No! Olivant shall not speak today! Not while I have power to lift my sword and men around me who are Franks!'

So the Saracen battalions broke over the reef of Frankish knights and swept many away. Horses clad in Frankish colours lay dead on top of their dead riders, and fallen shields bossed the ground.

Each man spent his life dearly, and took ten Saracen souls with him to the gates of death. Even so, when the third onslaught fell back, nothing more was left of Roland's defensive wall than a knot of fifty exhausted men.

'We have turned them! We have finished them!' exclaimed Roland, crimson from head to foot in the blood of his enemies.

As one man, the fifty lay down with a crash of buckled armour. They were too weary to raise a cheer. They had seen too many friends die to glory in their survival. A dozen vultures hopped and crouched within arm's reach, but no one had strength to shoo them away. Over the distant mountain ridges, the last of the column of retreating Frankish wounded moved out of sight. Roland watched them disappear with satisfaction.

Turning back, he saw, by the light of the low sun, another five battalions of Saracens closing in fast. Their numbers were as vast as the waves in the sea. They would wash over Roland's rearguard like the ocean over a handful of pebbles.

Fifty men looked at him with despair in their eyes. Fifty swords stabbed the ground, as the knights of Roland dragged themselves painfully to their feet once more.

Only then did Roland reach for his ivory horn. He placed it to his lips, and prayed for breath enough to blow it. He summoned the breath from the four winds, and he blew till his eyes and ears bled.

Olivant gave a blast which froze the Saracen horses in their tracks. Overhead in the sky, birds stricken by the note fell dead on to the helms of the advancing Moors. Elephants bellowed on the dusty plains of Africa, as if stirred by a memory. Boulders rolled and shattered, and the clodded mud shivered into sandy grains.

Roland's horse died beneath him, its great heart shrunk by the terrible noise. And the Horn Olivant – sounded a thousand times in victory – cracked and split in sounding defeat.

Twenty miles away, Charlemagne put his hands to his ears at the sound. He knew the Horn Olivant as well as the cry of his own baby son, as well as the echo of his own voice.

'Roland needs us!' he told his princes and dukes, his earls and knights.

They rode back through the brightly clothed squires, past the muddy foot soldiers, through the feathered ranks of archers, past the wagons and wagonboys. Their frenzied gallop startled the armourers and farriers, shook the machines and engines of war. The dead men slung across their saddles all but woke. The wounded and the sick shuffled aside to make room, for they too had heard the cry of Horn Olivant and knew that Roland was in need of help.

Too late did Charlemagne return to Roncesvalles. Too late did he counter the last Saracen attack. One hundred thousand of the enemy had finally overwhelmed the troops of Roland, and the finest of the Frankish chivalry lay like a field of flowers killed by frost.

Roland himself lay face up to the sky, beside him the Horn Olivant, like a crescent moon cradling the sun. Across his legs lay a Saracen banner, token of respect from one race of knights to another. At the sight of it, Charlemagne wept. 'Oh proud, proud Roland! Why did you wait so long to sound your horn?' asked the Emperor of his finest knight. But Roland said nothing in reply. The lips which had sounded Horn Olivant were silent now, and pale as ivory.

A Question of Life and Death

A GREEK MYTH

THE PEOPLE of Thebes grew lazy and selfish, and begrudged the things they had once given to the gods. They visited the temple of the sun god Apollo less and less often, left smaller and smaller offerings on the altar. One day, when he found nothing but a half-eaten apple and a sardine, where once there had been whole carcasses of beef, whole sheaves of flowers, he considered the time had come to remind Thebes of its duties to the gods. He sent a monster, a creature of hideous grace, of grotesque magnificence, to devour anyone who set foot outside the town.

The Sphinx – part woman, part lion, part eagle – made her lair above the main highway out of Thebes, couched on a ledge of rock. Whenever a traveller passed by, down she would leap, waving her lion's tail. The traveller, stricken with wonder as much as fear, would gaze up at the tumbling mane of black and gold fur, the soulful features, the gigantic wings raising the Sphinx rampant off the ground. Her shadow cast the whole valley into gloom.

'Answer me this riddle,' she demanded, in a voice as big as doom. 'Which animal has four legs in the morning, two in the afternoon, three in the evening, and is weakest when it has most?'

It was the kind of teaser that might go round at a party, or to pass the time on a journey. And yet no one who trod that road out of Thebes thought the riddle a small or trivial joke. It was a question of life or death. For when they guessed wrongly, the Sphinx tore them cloth from clothes, hair from head, limb from trunk, body from soul, and ate each piece.

Soon no one dared come to Thebes and no one dared leave. The Council sat to discuss the answer to the riddle. The townspeople huddled on street corners, their only conversation the Riddle of the Sphinx. Rewards were offered – the throne of Thebes and the hand of the newly widowed queen in marriage – and people reckless, or penniless, or cocksure enough, risked answering the Sphinx's riddle.

'Which animal has four legs in the morning, two in the afternoon and three in the evening and is weakest when it has most?'

'A giraffe!'

'A circus horse!'

'One of the constellations!'

No one returned to claim their reward.

'A centipede!'

'One of the gods!'

'A cockatrice!'

No one returned.

Then along came Oedipus. He approached Thebes one green morning – and was met by the Sphinx.

'Which animal has four legs in the morning, two in the afternoon and three in the evening, and is weakest when it has most?'

Oedipus shielded his eyes and looked up at the Sphinx, a woman of sumptuous beauty imprisoned in the body of a lion and given only wings to solace her. 'You are only a lion, and though the lion is called King of the Beasts, truly it is not: Man is that. You are only an eagle, and though you may fly high over the earth, you do not rule it: Man does that. You are only a woman, and though you may

have had men love, hate or fear you, you are powerless:
Man will always oppress you.'

'Answer my riddle!' demanded the Sphinx in a voice as
terrible as fate.

'I already have. A man crawls on all fours when he's a
baby, on two when he's grown, and leans on a stick in his
old age, when he's frail and toothless, "Man" is the answer
to your riddle, and Oedipus is the man who answered it.'

At that, the Sphinx gave a scream, like an eagle falling,
like a lion caught in a trap, like a woman vexed to the point
of desperation. She pounced at Oedipus – over Oedipus –
clearing his head with her lion's leap. Over the brink of a
gaping ravine she leapt. Her wings opened no more than a
book riffling its torn pages, for she had chosen to die on the
rocks below.

Thebes whooped with joy, opened its gates once more,
and made Oedipus King. Once again they made sacrifices
to Apollo and the gods who lived on Mount Olympus.
People hardly bothered to remember the answer to the
riddle, though they never forgot the Sphinx. Perhaps the
true Riddle of the Sphinx is not what she asked, but why
she asked it, and why the right answer drove her to such
despair.

The Harp of Dagda

AN IRISH MYTH

THEY CAME from the four great cities in the sky –
from Falias and Gorias, Finias and Murias. They
had studied every kind of knowledge at the feet of
the cities' Four Wise Kings, but their destiny was to live on
earth a while, a tribe like any other. So they came riding
down on the wind, hidden by magic clouds, and the home
they chose – for were they not the wisest of the wise? – was
Ireland. Their chieftain was Dagda, and they were like
giant gods to the wild men of the bogs and peat lakes. They
were the Good Men, the Dananns.

With them they brought the greatest treasure from each
of the four celestial cities: a stone from Falias, a sword
from Gorias, a spear from Finias and, from Murias, the
bottomless cauldron.

Even in times of famine, the Dagda's Magic Cauldron
was always full – of meaty soup, or porridge threaded with
golden honey – and no matter how many hungry people
dipped in their spoons, it was never emptied, never scraped
clean to the iron studs of its bulging belly. No wonder they
clamoured to make Dagda King of Ireland, too.

The Magic Stone was placed beneath the throne; and
when Dagda seated himself, it roared like a lion, as if to say,
'You have chosen aright. This is the true King.' No king was
chosen afterwards unless the stone shouted for him.

In battle the Magic Spear felled twenty men each time it
was thrown, and the Magic Sword melted whole ranks of
men where they stood.

But greater still than all these treasures was the Dagda's Harp and the Harpist who played it to him at the glimmering fireside. For men can fight their battles with bare hands if need be, and tighten their belts when they are hungry. But no civilized man can live without music and song.

Even the barbarian, spitting into the straw of his squalid hut, wants music to soothe him at the end of a long day's cruelty. That is why the King of the Fomorians set his heart on having the Harp of Dagda.

Nine winged Fomorian warriors flew down on the castle of the Dananns, like skuas mobbing the snowy gulls on the cliffs of Tyree. Shrieking and swooping, they seized the Harpist by his curly hair and lifted both him and his harp high into a stormy sky. The Dananns, rushing to the doorway, shaking their swords at the diminishing shapes in the wild sky, felt rain fall in their faces like the notes of a lament.

'This time the Fomorians have flown one league too far into the realms of wickedness,' said Dagda, his head brushing the roofbeams, his cloak extinguishing the fire. 'Come, Men of the Good, and we shall get back the Harp and the Harpist of Dagda!'

'Shall we strike them dead with the Magic Spear of Finias?'

'Shall we cut them in pieces with the Magic Sword?'

Dagda considered, and upon consideration dropped his voice to a murmur. 'No, children, no. For the Harp has soul enough to yearn for its home, and the Fomorians have too little soul to know the value of what they have. There will be no need to spill blood.'

Three men only, Dagda, Lugh and Ogma the Warrior, travelled to the Fomorian settlement. It took them some time, for they did not fly, but patiently picked their way over bog and heath, sheep track and stony stream till they saw a crooked pall of smoke rising from a crooked roof. The banqueting hall of the Fomorians was crammed with noise, but none was harp music. For the Harp refused to sound and the Harpist refused to play it, and no Fomorian had the art of making music. The King, after an outburst of spleen, had hung the Harp, along with his other hunting trophies, high on the wall.

When he saw the gigantic Dagda filling the doorway of the banqueting hall, he rubbed his smoke-reddened eyes and grinned. 'Come in! Come in!' he said, thinking to humiliate the Dananns still more with condescending shows of hospitality. 'Cooks! Prepare a bite for the great Dagda. You know what an appetite the man has!'

Three men with shovels set about digging a pit in the floor, a trough big enough to hold a horse. Then the cooks brought cauldrons full of porridge and vats full of milk, and slopped them into the pit until a steaming pond lay at Dagda's feet, looking more like a bath than a meal.

'Most kind,' said Dagda, graciously inclining his head. He pulled from his belt a spoon, or rather a ladle, its bowl so big that a man and woman could have cheerfully gone to bed in it and not fallen out till morning. In a matter of half a dozen spoonfuls, the porridge was gone, though Dagda stayed to scrape round the hole, supplementing his meal with a spoonful or two of gravel and earth.

While the Fomorians sat spellbound by this massive feat of eating, Dagda's eyes searched the smoky hall till they lit on the Harp. Under his breath he began to say,

'O come, my orchard of notes,
Strung with the four seasons of sound.
Come, you breath of spring,
you heat of summer,
you colours of autumn,
you stillness of winter.
Come, you bed of sweet sleep!

Come, you square for dancing!
Come, you weft of woven stories!
Come, you web of captured dreams!
Come, you magic, mouthless, marvellous, musical
*   man of mine!'*

The Harp sprang from the wall and plunged like a fish eagle. It cracked against the skulls of the nine Fomorians who had raided the Castle of Dagda, and their black wings sagged around them, moulting in the moment of death. Then it settled in the arms of Dagda, as gentle as Noah's dove returning to the ark.

As the room erupted in chaos, the Fomorian men diving for their swords, the women shrieking with terror, Dagda touched the strings of his harp and began to play – a hearty, happy tune. He smiled as he did so, and the Harpist, who had crept to his feet, smiled too. But the Fomorians did more than smile. They began to laugh! They could not help it. Their shoulders jigged and their big bellies quaked while they laughed just as though they had heard the funniest of jokes.

They held their sides and dabbed their eyes, and those who had half risen to kill the Dananns where they stood, rolled across the table in paroxysms of helpless laughter.

Dagda passed the harp to his son Ogma, who played in a different key – a sad, lilting lament like the grief of a dying swan. The laughing Fomorians, like children at bedtime who have over-excited themselves, burst into sudden hysterical tears. Their eyes streamed and their mouths gaped open, wailing and weeping till the dirty floor was slippery with tears.

Then Ogma handed the Harp to its harpist, who cradled it like a new-born baby and bent his head, low and loving, over the web of strings. The weeping Fomorians, despite their uncontrollable grief, had turned over the table and were starting to thrown aside the stools to lay hands on the three Dananns. Some had drawn swords, others spears which they raised overhead, preparing to impale the Good Men against the door.

But when the Harpist began to play, the foremost spear-wielder halted on one foot and leaned backwards. His wailing mouth stretched wider still into a monumental yawn. Then he keeled over backwards like a felled tree. Drunken with sudden sleepiness, the rest of the Fomorians reeled about, cannoning into one another and tumbling to the floor. Some slept propped in the corners, and one hung over the back of a chair.

The King simply rolled out of his throne and into the dogs' basket, where the hounds licked him curiously.

'Until we meet on the battlefield!' said Dagda to the sleeping Fomorians. 'For such is our fate.' Then he and his warriors closed the great doors softly behind them. The sound of snoring followed them all the way back to their castle.

The death of days and the tides of time wrought a change in the men called Good. When the world grew old and sour and villainous, like the Fomorians, the tribe of Good diminished – oh, not in wisdom or skill, but in actual physical stature. They shrank, just as the goodness of the world shrank, and changed their dwelling place once again, from earth to the places beneath the earth. They lived in the green mounds of the lonely places and changed – as the grub changes to a butterfly – into the faeries of Ireland.

And they took with them their treasures: the sword, the cauldron, the spear – all but the Magic Stone. Most certainly, they took Dagda's Harp. That is why, sometimes, you may see a man, all alone and quite without cause, suddenly laugh out loud, or weep into his sleeve, or sit down beneath a tree on a grassy mound and fall asleep with the ease of a child. He has heard the music, you see, coming from underground.

A Nest and a Web

A LEGEND FROM THE MIDDLE EAST

A T FIRST, when Muhammad preached, they said he was mad. But that is not uncommon in the experience of prophets. When his words began to be believed, then he was in far greater danger.

For Muhammad the prophet lived in Mecca, city of the idol-makers, who had charge of the house of the gods and made their money selling idols. In those days, the house of the gods in Mecca held three hundred and sixty idols depicting the gods of a multitude of different religions. People came from all over the pagan world to worship this god, or that goddess, and there was a great deal of money to be made from selling them goods and mementos of their pilgrimage.

But Muhammad spoke of only one God. 'Smash the pagan idols, empty God's house of them. Allah is the one, the only God.'

Now Muhammad was a man of good reputation, with great influence in the city. When he spoke, he fired the hearts of his listeners. He was called the One Who Can Be Trusted, for his fair dealing in business, and he dreamed dreams of the kind lesser men do not.

So the idol-makers trod carefully. 'We'll make you King of Mecca if only you will stop your preaching, Muhammad!' they said. 'Don't you see how this new religion of yours will damage the trade in idols and cut the revenue of the house of the gods?'

But Muhammad did not care about their greedy profits,

and he would not stop preaching what God had told him to preach. 'Allah is the one, the only God.'

When bribes did not work, the idol-makers used threats. 'We'll shun all your tribe and buy nothing from them in the marketplace. Perhaps they can put a stop to this foolishness of yours!'

But Muhammad would not stop his preaching. 'Allah is the one, the only God.'

Next, the idol-makers pretended to be tolerant. But Muhammad's following was growing; more and more people began to believe what he was saying. Muhammad knew that the idol-makers would resort to violence soon, to put a stop to him.

Some pilgrims from Medina, four hundred kilometres away, heard Muhammad preach – 'Allah is the one, the only God!' – and they delighted in his message. 'Come and preach in Medina!' they said. 'We want our friends, our families, our neighbours to hear you for themselves. Honour us with your presence! Leave behind Mecca and all those who hate you!'

So Muhammad left Mecca with his wife – left the city where he had grown up, left the house of the gods and the company of his tribe. And he walked out along a new road, into a new Chapter of his life's story.

Only in the nick of time did he leave. For assassins were on the streets that same night, with drawn knives, and murder in their hearts. 'Gone? Left to spread his lies further afield? He must be stopped!' The idol-makers were filled with bitter malice, and went after Muhammad, armed and on horseback, pursuing a pair of helpless travellers.

The ground shook to the gallop of hooves. When Muhammad looked round, the sun shone on naked swords and spear points. There was only one road, and the idol-makers intended to ride it till they rode down Muhammad and trampled his 'message' into the dust.

In a gorge, where the hot sun ricocheted from rock to rock, and the air melted and ran, Muhammad sought a hiding place. He found a cave a little way from the track, clambering over rocks and thorns to reach its dark mouth. He and his wife crept inside – it was cool, like a blessing – and crouched down, silent and still, in the rear of the cave.

But the galloping came closer with every second, and now the noise of voices, too – shouted commands, and swords slashing at the brambles. There was not the smallest chance that the cave would escape attention if the pursuers searched the gorge.

The horses came to a halt directly below. Men dismounted, and footsteps could be heard on the grassless ground. There was a rattle of stones as two soldiers clambered towards the mouth of the cave. Their silhouettes moved across the daylit entrance, and Muhammad's wife huddled closer, pressing her hands over her mouth in terror.

'Look here,' said one of the searchers, 'a pigeon's nest with a full brood of eggs in it.'

The second came to see, but chose not to count the little blue eggs for it would mean brushing his face against a massive spider's web. The web's geometric threads, strung with dewdrops, shimmered in the sunlight, the tapestried work of weeks by some industrious spider. It clad the cliff face and curtained the cave from portal to portal.

'Well, it's plain no one's been this way for a while,' said the soldiers, and turned back down the mountainside.

Muhammad's wife turned to her husband in amazement.

A web? A nest full of unbroken birds' eggs? How had she entered the cave without seeing them? How had they both entered the cave without breaking them? It was impossible, as the soldiers had rightly thought.

Muhammad was deep in prayer, facing towards the holy city he had left behind. His face was at peace, his praying hands steady, not shaking. 'Of course,' thought his wife.

Where was her faith that she had feared for their safety? Was not Allah great enough, resourceful enough to protect his own prophet from danger? Was it so incredible that Allah, who made the universe, should have spared the gift of a bird's nest and a spider's web to keep Muhammad and his message alive?

When the idol-makers had gone, Muhammad and his wife continued on their way towards Medina and a new life, breaking free of the past as pigeon chicks break free from their eggs. And eloquent Muhammad went on to weave a web of words which captured the hearts and souls of millions.

Ash

A NATIVE AMERICAN MYTH

A MAN HAD four sons, and three of them were his pride and joy. The fourth was his despair. Squat and ugly, he spent all day lolling by the fire, gazing into the flames, never stirring to do a useful day's work. 'What are you *doing* exactly?' his father would ask, losing patience.

'Just thinking.' His face was streaked with soot, his clothes grubby with sitting in the warm ashes: his brothers called him Ash. They called him a great many other, less flattering names, as well, and threw things at him – fish bones, apple cores, insults. But Ash hardly noticed. The flames' reflection danced in his bloodshot eyes, and he just went on thinking.

To the whole village, Ash was an idle layabout. They could not pass by without kicking him, could not talk about him without a sneer in their voices and a spit in his direction.

The young women went by giggling and chanting:

> *'Ash, Ash, go and hunt!*
> *Or is your hunting knife too blunt?*
> *Ash, Ash, make a wish!*
> *Wish you'd ever caught a fish?*
> *Ash, Ash, by the fire*
> *What made you so awful tired?*
> *Wasn't chasing girls, I bet'ya:*
> *Wouldn't know one if you met her!'*

Then one day the neighbouring tribe issued a challenge: 'Our champion will wrestle yours!'

Ash's brothers, like all the other young men, were thrilled, glad of the excitement, eager to be chosen champion of the tribe . . . until they saw their opponent. Whale Man was as big as a hut and as heavy with blubber as a bull seal. He came through the woods breaking down saplings and knocking bears out of the trees. He picked up a newly carved canoe and threw it like a paper dart, so that it wedged in a mudbank. Then, bellowing like a moose, he kicked a hole in the side of the village long house rather than go in through the door.

'Who's it going to be? Whose head shall I rip off today?'

There was a long wait for volunteers.

The village squirmed with shame. The chieftain pondered how many sealskins he must give his neighbours, to make them go away and take their champion with them.

'I'll fight you,' said Ash, standing up. 'You've put out the fire anyway, with your big feet. So I may as well fight you, to keep warm.'

The giant wrestler began to laugh. The women began to laugh with him, to be polite, and then the men joined in, hoping the giant had a sense of humour. Ash? Wrestle?

'You? You couldn't wrestle your way out of a hammock!' hissed his brothers. 'Keep quiet; you'll make things worse!'

But Ash simply ducked out through the hole in the wall, waited for Whale Man to follow, and then took hold of him by both feet. Ash shook Whale Man like a blanket, till the fleas flew out of his hair, then beat him like a drum, till the stains flew off his loincloth. Ash whirled him about by his ears, and flung him into the next valley where he landed with a noise like rotten fruit. When the chief looked around, the challengers were nowhere to be seen.

'Wow!' he exclaimed.

'Fluke,' said one brother.

'Lucky accident,' said another.

'Trick of the light,' said the third.

But Ash had gone back indoors, anyway, and stretched himself out beside the newly built fire. No one mentioned the matter of the giant again, and he never reminded them.

There was magic in Ash. He must have read it in the embers, or dreamed it in a dream. But somehow there was magic in Ash, and his fellow men chose to ignore it. Magic does not like to be ignored.

Early one morning, a woman emerged from the long house, on her way to fetch water. She looked at the skyline and gave a shriek. For lumbering towards her, larger than any giant, were all the trees of the distant forests – on the warpath.

From every side came trees, roots clawing up the soil, knotting their branches into fists, their heads tossing with indignation. 'We're surrounded! We're done for!' cried the villagers, clinging to one another. 'They'll trample us into the ground!'

Not until the trees were shoulder to shoulder, their branches interlocking, their trunks as close as the bars of a cage, did Ash stir from beside the fire. He stepped to the door of the hut, peered blearily against the bright light, and shouted: 'Stop it! Go back! There's no harm done! My word on it!'

The trees faltered and came to a halt. Their dark green tops bent over Ash, like parents bending anxiously over an injured child. Fir cones fell by the hundred on the long house roof. Then the trees spun round on their roots and trudged away. With the wind soughing through their green needles, they sounded like grumpy whisperers.

'That was a narrow escape,' said Ash's father.

'Near thing,' said his brother.

'Did you hear Ash?' said a second. 'Who did he think he was shouting at? Does he really think he made the trees go?'

'Must be even madder than we thought,' said the third.

The ground rumbled and the sky shook. The villagers, dawdling back to their work, looked up and saw – no, it could not be – the smallest of changes in the familiar view. The horizon did not seem quite the same shape, the mountains not quite as they had been before.

But the ground rumbled and the sky continued to shake. By noon, they realized the dreadful truth – that the far-off mountains were no longer far away. They had picked up their skirts of grass, flexed their bones of rock and were moving, purple-headed with anger, across the coastal plain. Where their shoulders rubbed together, sparks flew, and from their clenched fists, boulders tumbled in avalanches of rage.

You see, there was magic in Ash, and magic does not like to be ignored.

Larger and larger loomed the mountains, closing in on every side, while the villagers ran this way and that, but found no escape.

'Ash! Ash! Come out and speak to them! Tell them to stop! Ask them not to crush us! Help us, do!' they begged, but Ash only lazed beside the fire, watching the magic of the flames as usual. At last he got to his feet, went outside, and held up both hands. 'Peace. Stand still. That's far enough.'

Obedient as dogs, the mountains lay down where they were, jostling, settling, lounging along the ground, the evening sun on their watching faces. This time, when Ash lay back down in his favourite place, the girls brought him food, his brothers brought him drink, and his father threw more wood on the fire.

Now they saw the magic in Ash, his family and tribe stopped calling him a layabout and a fool. Suddenly they were as proud to have him in their midst as any champion wrestler or holy man, and spoke of him boastfully: 'We have a man full of magic! The trees and mountains do as he tells them! We have a man who can think all day, without tiring! If only we had his wisdom. If only we had his magic in us!'

One day, visitors came calling. Six men got out of a fine carved canoe and walked up to the village.

'Greetings. Have you come to buy sealskins?' said the villagers, but the strangers answered not a word.

'Have you come in peace? Or to challenge us to wrestle?' said the villagers, but the strangers answered not a word.

'Have you come looking for bribes? Or warriors? Or craftsmen? Or fishermen?'

But the strangers simply walked straight ahead into the long hut and up to the fire where Ash lay thinking.

'I have been expecting you,' said Ash, looking up at once. Instead of flames dancing in his eyes, they had become strangely blue, the colour of water. 'Is your master ill?'

'He is, young man, and if we do not hurry, he may die before we get back to him. Please come.'

Ash got up and strode down to the canoe with them. He climbed aboard and took up an oar, and his powerful arms helped speed the boat out to sea.

Not far from the horizon, where the setting sun gouged a blood-red whirlpool in the sea, the canoe spun round three times, and sank out of sight.

Standing tiptoe on the shore, the young women wept and Ash's father wrung his hands. 'Death had sent an escort for him! Death has taken away our magical young man!'

But the six messengers were not from Death. They came from the sea caves beneath the setting sun, sent by the strongest man of all. When the canoe touched bottom, all seven got out and began to walk. Rays swam by like blankets on a high wind. Dogfish cruised the canyons of weed-hung rock. The sunlight filtered, in a frail dapple, through the choppy surface of the sea, lighting a silver storm of salmon. Across the sea floor, the six messengers led Ash to a deep sea trench. And there, on a bed of sea grass, lay a man so old that his body was more spirit than flesh. It seemed that some monstrous torturer had skewered him to the bed of the sea, for a huge pole stood on his chest, soaring high, high out of view.

'Ah! You have come at last! At last I may rest. At last!' sighed the frail old man, lifting his head a little. 'For a thousand years I have held up the sky with this pole. For a thousand years, my strength has been equal to the task. But now I am old and dying, and there is no one but you with magic enough in your soul and strength enough in your breast to balance this pole in my place.'

Ash at once lay down beside the old man, and took the end of the pole, resting it on his own chest. The soot that had always stained his face had washed clean away. The smuts that had always dirtied his clothes floated away on the tide.

'I am asking much of you, Spotless One,' said the weary old man. 'What will you do, as the years wash the rocks into sand? What will you do to pass the time away?'

'Oh, that will be no hardship to me,' Spotless One replied. 'I do not know the meaning of boredom. I shall simply lie here and watch the magic of sunlight dancing on the wave tops. And that will help me think.'

The Tower of Babel

A HEBREW MYTH

EARLY in the morning of the world, before the human race had grown very large at all, it moved all together, one great tribe of wandering nomads pitching their tents where dusk overtook them.

Then one day, in one year, they decided to exchange tents for houses of stone, and they built a city in the centre of a great plain, and stopped their wandering. When the city was built, they were very proud of it – overly proud of it, for its gateways and market squares, its staircases and turrets convinced them, 'There's nothing we can't do! Let's build a tower as high as Heaven itself, so that people half a world away will see it and wonder!' So they baked bricks and they mixed mortar and they built up . . . and up and up.

When God saw their tower growing, and their pride growing along with the tower, he did not like the idea of the people of Babel reaching so far upwards. So he stamped once, and the ground trembled. He breathed once, and the mortar dried to dust and bled from between the bricks. He took one brick from the base of the Tower of Babel, and it fell. Like Satan falling on his belly in the dust, the Tower of Babel tumbled, and with it the pride and ambition of its builders. Clutching each other, clutching at limbs of wood and lintels of stone, they plummeted to the ground, rolling and bowling in every direction across the great plain.

And when they opened their mouths to bemoan the disaster, strange words came from between their lips, strange accents and dialects. Tugging at one another's coats, gesticulating with frantic hands, they yelled in each other's faces. But one man could not make sense of what his neighbour said to him; one woman could not make the woman beside her understand.

The great city was never finished. The Tower of Babel was never rebuilt. For with human beings split and divided by differences of language, they found it very hard to work, or even to think, in harmony.

They have never learned the trick of it, not in all these years.

Saint Christopher

A EUROPEAN LEGEND

CHRISTOPHER was born neither good nor bad, but he knew his worth. 'I'm strong, I'm tall, I can turn my hand to most things. I shall work for only the best. I shall take for my master the most powerful ruler in the world.' So he went down to Hell, to serve the Devil, because he had heard that more people feared the Devil than any other emperor or tyrant. Certainly the Devil's banners were to be seen flying everywhere on Earth.

At the door of Hell, there was a long queue of people wanting to sign in the Devil's service. At last Christopher and one other man were admitted into the presence of the Lord of Darkness, who sat on a throne of fire, eating sparks.

'Swear to obey me in all things,' said the Devil (which was the way of masters and servants in those days).

'What should I swear by?' asked the other applicant. 'By my mother? On my life? By Jesus Christ?' At the mention of Christ's name, the Devil gave a shudder, and his red eyes rolled. Christopher had sudden misgivings. Quickly, he made the sign of the Cross – he had often seen Christians do it – touching his forehead, chest, then each shoulder. Sure enough, the Devil leapt out of his chair and ran. 'Don't do that! Don't! If you're going to work for me, don't ever do that, d'you hear?'

'Work for him?' thought Christopher, as the Devil slammed the chamber door. 'I set out to work for the most powerful master in the world. Plainly this Jesus Christ is more powerful.'

So he made it his business to find out all about Jesus. And he liked what he heard.

'What must I do to serve this Jesus Christ?' he asked a priest.

'Serve your fellow men. Either by prayer, as a monk, or by making yourself useful to those in need.'

'You mean I don't get to meet him? Not meet my own master?'

'Not in this life, Christopher. In this life you will only see Christ's face in the faces of the poor and needy.'

Now Christopher was not of a nature suited to a monk's life, so he decided to make himself useful in some practical way. He built himself a hut beside a river, and whenever travellers needed to cross over, he carried them across the river on his strong shoulders. Whole families of eight and nine children he could carry, though the current was strong and the river cold and wide. As he carried them, he would listen to their sad stories, and make the children laugh and the adults brighten, while he sang a song or told a fable.

One day, a little boy came to the river. 'I want to cross over,' he said.

Christopher swung him on to his shoulders as a swimmer might hand a towel round his neck, and broke into a cheerful song.

But a short way out from the shore, he had to stop singing. The boy was much heavier than he looked. 'I must be getting old,' he told his passenger. 'I've carried ten of your size before now, without thinking twice!'

Halfway across the river, the child began to feel even heavier. Christopher could hardly lift his head or straighten his back. 'What age did you say you were, boy?' But the boy did not reply.

With every step, the boy grew heavier, so that soon Christopher could barely keep his footing. The river shoved at him, and the weight on his back bore down like a bale of wool, a full barrel, a hod of bricks. He staggered and gasped for breath. His mouth was being pushed under, his nose too. He had either to let go of the boy or drown. He turned his face towards the sky and took a last gulp of air. 'I fear, son, that I cannot . . .'

And yet he must. How could he let a child drown whom he had offered to carry? He must get the boy to the shore, even if it cost him his last ounce of strength. The river swamped him. The boy's hand, clutched in his hair, seemed to be plucking out his brain, and yet he plunged on, his face submerged now, his lungs bursting. In his heart, he prayed: not to live, but that the boy should not drown.

At last, his feet felt shallower ground and he crawled up the bank on all fours and dropped on his face beneath the boy.

'Thank you,' said the child, 'but I have no money to pay you.'

Christopher did not want to frighten him by saying how close they had both come to drowning, so he simply rolled on to his back, smiled through his sodden beard, and said what he always said. 'No charge, son. I did it for Christ.'

'You speak truer than you know,' said the boy in a deep, musical voice, then ran away, fast as a deer, across the wooded landscape.

Christopher lay on his back looking up at the sky. And when he had breath enough to speak what he had realized, he shouted up at the birds: 'No wonder he weighed so much! I wasn't carrying a child – I was carrying the greatest man in the world! I met Jesus today, and carried him on my back!'

And that is why travellers pray to Saint Christopher for a safe journey, because everyone needs kindness from those they meet on a journey, a helping hand, a glimpse of Christ's smile on the face of a stranger.

God Moves Away

A MYTH FROM TOGO

'I TELL you God lives above the sky. Way up high. Out of earshot almost. We know about these things in Togo.'

'Are you saying God never lived on Earth, among men?'

'Not at all. Of course he did! The sky hung about here, not much higher than a man's head, and God used it for a hammock. But he moved away. Don't you know that? Don't you know why?'

'I know you're going to tell me.'

People were disrespectful, yes. Little children used to wipe their greasy paws on the sky at the end of a meal, and cooks used to tear pieces off, for the cooking pot. I hear it was delicious – gave you wind, but it was delicious.

You know how the women pound corn into meal in this part of the world? With a big wooden bowl to hold the grain, and a huge wooden pestle for pounding it? Bang, bang, bang. Well, naturally the pestle needs to thump down on the corn as hard as possible. So this old lady used to throw the pestle high in the air. It was made from a tree trunk and was as tall as she was, but she could thump that pestle up and down for hours on end, like an elephant stomping on peanuts. And of course every time she threw the pestle upwards, it used to catch God a fourpenny whack somewhere painful. One day it hit him in the eye.

That made him so mad that he packed up and left. He

—— 45 ——

did! Rolled up the sky and flew right up high, rubbing his eye and muttering.

Of course it was a help to the old woman's work, but a great sadness to everyone else. No more sky in the cooking pot. Nowhere to wipe their greasy hands. And – worst of all – it made a conversation with God so difficult. So hard to make him hear our prayers. So hard to take an argument before him for his judgement.

The old woman did what she could to make amends. She told her children and her grandchildren and every other greasy-handed child in the village to gather up all the pounding bowls.

Some still had corn in. Some had rainwater slopping about in the bottom. Some were old and bruised with fifty years of pounding. But the old lady piled them up, one on top of the next, and climbed up, to ask God if he wouldn't come back down where he belonged.

She nearly made it, too. When she reached the top of the pile and was balanced in the topmost bowl, like an egg in an eggcup, she could almost reach the hem of God's robe. She stood on tiptoe. She hopped as high as she dared, but it made the tower wobble alarmingly.

'One more bowl and I'm there!' she called down to her children. But there were no bowls to be had. 'I know!' she called. 'Take the bottom one out and pass it up to me. Then I'll be able to reach!'

And that is what they did, for it is a foolish child who argues with his grandmother. They took away the bottom pounding bowl – *wobble, clatter, eeek!* – and though the old lady made a snatch for the hem of God's robe, she missed. And that was that.

Wilhelm Tell

A SWISS LEGEND

'TO LIFE, Liberty and a free Switzerland!' That was
the toast they drank and the oath they swore in
secret. But in public, few dared to defy the tyranny
of the Austrian Empire. So they paid the heavy taxes, they
obeyed the unfair laws, and in secret they dreamed of
independence and swore grand oaths, to keep from
despairing.

Wilhelm Tell was different. A farmer from a remote
mountain farm, he spoke little and thought deeply. So
when he swore such an oath, the words dropped like hot
sealing wax on to a deed of law, and made those who heard
him tremble at the strength of his feelings.

In every respect, Tell was the best of men: best archer,
best mountaineer, best helmsman at a boat's tiller out on
Lake Lucerne; best friend to have when a friend was
needed; best father in all the world, as far as his son Carl
was concerned. Many suspected that, since the Austrians
had come to power, a temper burned like volcanic lava in
Tell's breast, but his friends and family had never seen it
flare. It was that family of his which kept Wilhelm at one
remove from the politics of rebellion. Only a bachelor can
afford reckless exploits in the name of Liberty; a married
man has other lives than his own to consider.

One cruelty gave the Austrian overlords a taste for
another and another. Men like Baron Gessler delighted in
inventing new humiliations to inflict on the Swiss. An edict
forbade any farmer the use of a horse or ox to pull his

plough. The farmer could haul his own plough, couldn't he, and give the horse and ox to his Austrian betters.

Baron Gessler stalked the streets and lanes, surrounded by bodyguards, to glory in the misery he caused. In fact, power was making Gessler a little peculiar, a little wild at the eye, a little unpredictable in his extravagant malice. He placed various of his hats on poles and sent them into the market square of every village, demanding that everyone who passed by must bow to the hat, as though to its owner. Soldiers were posted at the foot of each pole, to ensure everyone complied with the decree.

Old men with arthritic joints were obliged to bend their aching knees to Gessler's hat. Young women carrying babies, farmers laden with bales of hay were called on to pay their respects to the silly hat on high. Milkmaids could not sell their milk in the marketplace until they had curtseyed to Gessler's hat. From the window of an inn in Altdorf, Gessler himself watched, grinning, and thought of the same scene being acted out all over the canton.

It so happened that Wilhelm Tell chose that day to come to town for supplies. Nothing was farther from his mind than to make trouble: he had brought his dear son Carl with him. But no one had told him about the business of Gessler's hat, and as he crossed the square, one of the soldiers suddenly barked like a rabid dog, 'Bow to the hat, why don't you?'

'Why would I bow to a hat?' enquired Tell in his low, shy voice.

'Because it's the hat of Baron Gessler, and it represents him.'

Wilhelm squinted up at the hat. 'It might bear a passing resemblance to him, I suppose, if he ate less . . . But the day I bow to a hat is the day I grow ears and bray like a donkey. Bow to it yourself.'

With the bang of a door and the breaking of a beer mug, Baron Gessler came bellying out of the inn. A gobbet of chewed apple flew from his mouth as he blared. 'So! You refuse to obey my decree, do you? I've heard of you! You're Wilhelm Tell! I know all about you! You're famous hereabouts, aren't you? People never stop talking about you – what a good archer! what a great mountain-eer! And you're a dissident, are you? A subversive? A rebel?'

Suddenly guards were clinging to Tell like squirrels to a tree.

'That's a lot to accuse me of, simply because I insulted your hat,' said Tell calmly.

'So will you bow to it?'

'No.'

Gessler burst into hysterical laughter which puffed out his cheeks and made his forehead red. 'Then your farm's forfeit! I'll lock you up! I'll have you sent to Castle Kussnacht and . . .' Tell's grey eyes looked back at him, cold and unmoved. Gessler racked his brains for something more original in the way of cruelty. The longer Tell retained his dignity here in this public square, Gessler was the one being made to look small. He peered beyond Tell and saw something which inspired his malicious imagin-ation . . . 'Unless . . . '

Tell flexed his arm muscles, which were growing un-comfortable. A guard slithered to the ground. 'Unless?' he asked, peaceably.

'I hear you've a fair art with a crossbow. What a waste it would be to bury such talent in a dungeon!' Gessler looked down at the remains of the apple he had been eating. 'If you can shoot through this apple at a distance of one hundred paces, you can go free.'

'Agreed!' said Tell, taken aback by such uncharacteris-tically good sportsmanship.

Gessler hiccuped with laughter. 'Guards. Balance this apple on the head of Tell's son, and stand him in front of that tree yonder. That should help make Herr Wilhelm shoot straight!'

Up until that moment, Tell had been so intent on keeping his temper that he had forgotten entirely about Carl, about his little boy standing so still and wide-eyed in his father's long shadow. For the first time Gessler saw the flicker of fear he so loved to inflict. Tell was afraid to make the shot. He would crumble now, in front of all his admiring neighbours, and beg for mercy.

Nobody moved for a long time. Nobody moved until Carl reached out, took the half-eaten apple out of Gessler's hand and set off towards the tree. Along the shore of the lake he walked. One hundred paces? It was more like one hundred and fifty. Carl rested his back against the trunk and looked back at his father, so small now in the distance. 'You can do it, Father!' he called. His high sweet voice rang out as clear as a bell.

The soldiers tied Carl to the tree with ropes. They made as if to blindfold him, too. 'I won't flinch, if that's what you think,' he told them. 'I know my father can hit the apple.'

So he saw the huge crowd that had gathered seemingly from nowhere. He saw his father's face above the level crossbow – pale as snow on the mountaintops. He saw the sun flaring on the water of the lake a blinding brightness. He saw the metal bolt glint in the sun, the flash of a second one held between his father's fingers. Carl held his breath. A cloud covered the sun.

The bolt flew so fast that the twang of the bowstring and thud of the impact were like a single sound. A woman in the crowd screamed, '*You murderer, Gessler!*', for she had seen, through her fingers, an explosion of white and red as the bolt struck.

But it was only the apple splattering to pulpy pieces. Fragments stuck to the boy's hair, juice trickled into his eyes, as he smiled back at his father. Then a cheer went up from the Swiss crowd that was repeated at every window, shouted down every alleyway in Altdorf: '*He did it! Tell hit the apple!*'' Gessler, blustering and foolish, groped for something disparaging to say. 'Not so cocky, really, were you, Tell? Thought it might take two shots?' He pointed out the second bolt between Tell's fingers.

The archer shrugged. 'Oh yes, I thought my first bolt might kill my son. That's why I had a second ready for you, Gessler.'

'*Arrest him! Seize him! Traitor! Villain! Assassin!*' Gessler ducked behind a member of his bodyguard, his heart leaping with a mixture of terror and triumph, a cold sweat running down his fat neck. 'Your own words condemn you! Take him to Castle Kussnacht and let him wait in a dungeon for the headman's axe!'

A murmur like a hive of bees stirred among the crowd. Then an egg hit the back of Gessler's coat, a hail of pebbles began to fly. If Gessler had wanted to upset the people of Altdorf, he had surely succeeded, for they began to herd forward, like cattle roused by lightning.

'Run, Carl! Run!' cried Tell, and Carl picked up his heels and ran into the shelter of the crowd, which swallowed him up, hid him as surely as if he were invisible.

Arrest Tell? When he had won his freedom like that? Some injustices can be borne, some wickednesses tolerated. But this time Gessler had touched a nerve already rubbed raw by his tyranny. Someone smashed a market stall and began handing out sticks of wood for weapons. Some drew the money from their pockets – worthless Austrian coppers good for nothing but pelting worthless Austrians.

'It's no good, sir. We'll never reach the horses!' shouted the captain of the guard. 'Best get offshore. That's our only hope.' And so they beat an undignified retreat, jogging along a jetty, bundling Tell aboard a small fishing boat. The crowd also broke into a run, shaking their sticks and shouting, 'Get Gessler! Let's put a stop to him once and for all!'

'Steer, won't you?' Gessler pushed a sergeant in the chest.

'B-but I don't know how to —'

'Just do it, fool, before this rabble tears us limb from limb!'

As the space widened between boat and shore, Gessler crowed like a cock. 'Just wait till my *real* troops arrive!' he sneered at the people ranged along the jetty. '*You'll wish you'd never been born!*'

A sudden yaw in the boat made him stagger, and he cursed the helmsman. Then he saw the cause: a storm like a genie summoned from a bottle. Lake Lucerne, too, was rising up against tyranny and injustice.

There were blades of cold and arrows of ice in the wind. They sheered through the rigging and brought down the topsails on to the men below. The unwilling helmsman cowered in the bottom of the boat pleading for the help of a real sailor. 'Free Tell! He knows boats. He can sail anything! Free Tell or *we'll all drown*!'

'So even you admire the lout!' fumed Gessler. His opulent, fur-lined coat was so heavy with rain and spray that his knees were bowing. 'All right. All right! Cut the dog loose.'

The moment his hands were untied, Tell took the tiller of the boat and turned her into the wind. She stopped rolling and pitching and taking in water, and beyond that no one cared where she was heading. Minutes later, they saw the shore dead ahead, spines of jagged rock clawing the waves into an open wound of breaking water, a foaming maelstrom. They stared open-mouthed, letting the driving rain trickle down their throats. Did Tell mean to wreck the boat and take his enemies with him to the bottom of the lake?

At the last second, Tell swung on the tiller, and every

man aboard was sent sprawling. The prow reared up like a horse's head, the keel grazed bottom. The boat swung round within its own length, so that it was stern-on to the rock. And from the stern transom leapt Wilhelm Tell – out across a gulf of rioting water, black, deep and deadly. It was a phenomenal leap – a mountain goat's leap from one crag to the next. Only a mountaineer could have made it and held his balance on landing. Only the bravest could have made it in the teeth of a gale, while the wavetops gnashed and the foam flew like blinding snow. Only Wilhelm Tell could have done it with an iron crossbow slung across his back, snatched from the slippery deck the moment before he jumped.

The Austrian guards clung desperately to the boat rail, unwilling to let go despite Gessler's ranting: '*Shoot him! Shoot the villain! Kill him! Don't let him get away, Devil curse you!*'

The boat had the wind behind it now, and was driven out towards the centre of the lake, ropes snaking, sail ripping, and the tiller unmanned. On the shore, clambering agilely over the razor-sharp rocks a figure lithe as an otter reached the safety of dry land.

'I'll see you in Hell for this!' bawled Gessler. 'You so-called soldiers! You and your wives and sweethearts! I'll finish Tell! I'll burn down his farm with his wife and brat inside! I'll burn down every farm on the mountain! I'll burn down Altdorf!' The wind dropped suddenly, as if out-brayed by Gessler's cursing. The rain teemed blackly, but the drifting boat ceased her pitching as the storm stood still in horror.

The figure on the shore laid a single bolt to his crossbow and took aim. A furlong of darkness crammed with rain; half a moon, and all his breath used up. Tell fired. And the insane ranting stopped even more suddenly than the wind's howl had done.

Next morning found the boat adrift in the heart of Lake

Lucerne. The soldiers aboard, when asked what had become of the Baron, only pointed over the side at the still, secretive waters. Lake Lucerne is deep. It takes time to give up its captives. But the fishermen of the lake said that a great many fish died that night, as if poisoned by some pollution of the water.

The Swiss will only stand for just so much. They may bend to circumstance. They may bear with misfortune. But ultimately, they are slaves to no one. Within half a handful of years, Switzerland was free of Austria. It has never given up its independence since.

A Heart of Stone

A GREEK MYTH

'LOVE,' said the King, 'has never troubled me, I'm glad to say.' In fact, King Pygmalion of Cyprus had done rather better than simply not falling in love. He had managed to loathe women, with a deep and deadly loathing, ever since he had been able to tell them apart from men. 'Can't see the purpose of them,' he would say, in a superior way. 'Don't hunt elephants. Don't quarry rocks . . .'

If these seem strange virtues to set any great store by, it should be explained that Pygmalion was a sculptor as well as a king. His notion of true joy was a tusk of ivory or a block of marble, uncut, awaiting the touch of his chisel. He carved animals, heroes, children, pillars . . . and superbly, too. People could almost forgive him his hatred of women when they saw the genius of his carvings.

Venus did not forgive so easily. The Goddess of Love took great exception to his rude and ignorant remarks. Every day, from the slopes of Mount Olympus where the gods of Greece made their home, she could hear the supercilious voice of Pygmalion complaining: how women *talked*, how women *lied*, how women *spent money*, how women were a useless and troublesome invention he could well do without. Not surprisingly, he had never offered up a single sacrifice in the Temple of Venus. One day Venus stamped her foot, and her green eyes flashed with resolve. 'It is time, Pygmalion, to teach you a lesson!'

A stranger knocked at the door of Pygmalion's studio

next day – a tall hooded stranger with piercing green eyes.

'Greetings, your majesty. I am a traveller returned from foreign parts where I learned of a contest which might interest you. The King of Crete is offering a laurel wreath for the finest sculpture submitted. I thought of you at once, O King, knowing you to be the finest sculptor in the world.'

'Thank you! I shall carve a bull!' exclaimed Pygmalion, already selecting the ideal block from among the marble stacked in the yard . . . 'The Cretans like nothing better than a charging . . .'

'No, no!' interrupted the stranger. 'The statue must be of a woman. The one considered the most beautiful will be the winner.'

'Oh, but I never . . .'

But when Pygmalion turned round, there was no one to be seen.

Bravely overcoming his disgust, Pygmalion decided to compete nevertheless, and to carve a female figure. He chose the finest marble, sharpened his best tools and asked himself what could possibly make a *woman* seem beautiful. 'A wide, generous mouth,' he thought, 'but not always talking. A pair of large, tender eyes looking only at me. Hair flowing like the weed in a river, fit to drown a man . . .'

The figure which emerged from under his skilful fingers was tall and willowy, bending a little forward. She seemed to be listening with intent interest to everything Pygmalion had to say. 'I think you will do very nicely,' he found himself saying aloud to the sweetly inclined head, as he set down his tools. 'For a woman, you are really quite . . . quite . . . exquisite, if I do say so myself.' But the statue only looked back at him, with white marble eyes and a sweet but brittle smile.

When the King went to bed that night, he could not get the statue out of his mind. It was his best achievement yet, no doubt about it. It was perfect. He had to get up and go back to the studio just to look at it, at her. For the rest of the night he sat there, gazing at her, enthralled by a beauty of his own making.

Next morning he found himself unwilling to crate up his statue and despatch her to Crete. No sooner were the nails banged home than he prised them out again and recovered his masterpiece from the crate, setting her on a plinth where the sunlight flattered her lovely figure, her delicate features, her long curling hair. 'I shall call you Galatea,' he said, but her carved mouth did not respond, either to agree or disagree. She seemed more beautiful every time he looked at her, but cold and still. She seemed on the very point of moving – and yet she would never move. She was only a statue, after all.

For a week, Pygmalion did not leave his studio. His servants brought meat and drink to the door, but he sent them away. His ministers could get no answer to their knocking. They gathered round the door, anxious, worried. Then, when he did finally emerge, he rushed past them, white-faced, and ran all the way to the Temple of Venus on the hill, falling on his knees in front of the altar.

'O Goddess of Love, take pity on me! I'm a fool, I know it! I'm half-mad, I see that! But I can't help myself! I love her! I've fallen in love with my own statue! I deserve to be laughed at in the street – "There goes that fool who lost his heart to a piece of marble!" – but I never knew what it was like before. I never even guessed love could be like this! Pity me, goddess! Take this pain from my heart, this madness out of my brain! I'll carve your statue at every crossroads – if only you'll end this *pain*!'

His voice rang around the cavernous temple. The only faces looking down at him were images of the goddess Venus – tall, enthroned in a sea shell, clothed in locks of hair, carved in pallid stone.

He walked back to the studio, scuffing the heels of his

sandals. He might have gone to his palace, but the statue drew him, as a magnet draws iron. He must see it again, even though seeing it only increased his suffering, because it could never be anything but cold, insensible marble.

The look on his face was so terrible that his ministers and servants stepped back and did not try to speak to him. Pygmalion closed the door behind him and leaned against it, his eyes tight shut in self-loathing. 'Oh, what I'd give to be one of those lucky men I used to make fun of – in love with some dancer or priestess or orange-seller!'

'Are you speaking to me?'

He opened his eyes and saw at once that his statue was missing, his beloved statue. '*Where is she? What have you done with my statue?*' The stranger sitting in the seat by the window was so blotted out by the sunlight behind her that he saw only a dark shadow. But when she stood up – 'I'm sorry, what statue?' – he could see her more clearly: a beauty in green drapery and gold sandals, her hair falling in ringlets to front and back of her shoulders.

'I believe I may be a little unwell,' she said, in a sweet apologetic voice, 'for I cannot entirely remember how I came to be here. My name is . . .'

'Galatea,' said Pygmalion at once.

'That's right. How did you know? Or are we acquainted? You do seem rather familiar . . . if only I could remember. But I mustn't keep you from your work. I see you are a very fine sculptor, and I know how artists need peace and quiet.'

Thus Venus gave Pygmalion his perfect woman, satisfied that he had learned his lesson. Besides, she was extremely eager to see those statues he had promised to carve of her standing at every crossroads.

If the gods have one weakness, it is probably their vanity.

Babushka

A RUSSIAN LEGEND

T HE STAR shone – but then everything in Babushka's house shone, bright and glistening. So that when she glimpsed the new star shining in at the corner of the window, she saw nothing unusual in that. Everyone else in the village was out of doors, pointing and prattling. But Babushka would never waste her time so frivolously. She had a house to keep clean, washing and washing-up to do, weeding and kneading. She was too busy for wonders.

'A new star! See?'

'Never there before!'

'Last night it was over yonder.'

'It's moving!'

'Shifting!'

'Shining!'

'Amazing!'

'Wonderful!'

But Babushka was too busy for wonders.

She heard the new commotion in the street, too, the children ooh-ing and aah-ing, the herrumph of camels and the jingling of bridle bells.

'See their turbans!'

'See their cloaks!'

'Seethe scrolls and scriptures in their saddlebags!'

But nothing could make Babushka break off from her work until that knock at the door.

'May we rest here tonight, Babushka?' Three travellers stood in her neat little garden; their camels were tethered by the gate. Their clothes were dirty with the dust of many miles, but not so dusty that she could not see the quality and richness of their foreign weave.

'You'd best come in, sirs,' said Babushka in a shy whisper, 'though if you'd wipe your feet on the mat I'd be grateful.'

She bustled about fetching them cheese and milk, dates and nuts, bread and little cakes.

'Sit down and talk to us, Babushka,' said her visitors, but Babushka never sat down. There was far too much to do – especially with visitors in the house. There were blankets to be fetched for their beds, fires to be lit, apples to be polished for their dessert.

After dinner, the three foreign gentlemen, Caspar, Melchior and Balthazar, opened out maps on the table and discussed where their journey was taking them. 'We are following the new star,' they explained, when she brought them extra candles. 'It's leading us to the realm of a new king.'

'A new king. Fancy!' said Babushka, but she was too busy washing up the supper things to say more.

'The Christ of the Scriptures!' said Caspar. 'The Saviour of the World! The star marks his coming – is writing it in the sky!'

'The Saviour of the World? Well, God bless us!' said Babushka.

'We're taking him presents,' said Melchior. 'Gold and spices and rich ointments.'

'Fortunate man,' said Babushka.

'No, no! Only a baby as yet,' Balthazar corrected her. 'A newborn king!'

'Then may he live long, for his mother's sake,' said Babushka and the three turned quickly and looked at her, simply because at last she had stopped stock-still. She stood by the door, her shawl clutched close at her throat. 'I had a child once,' she said, 'but he died.' Then seeing the pity in their faces, she put on a bright smile and set off once more, straightening the ornaments, plumping the cushions, sweeping crumbs from under the table. 'No great matter. I keep busy, Children! They make a house untidy anyway.'

'Come with us, Babushka,' said Caspar.

'Come where, sir?'

'Yes, come with us tomorrow,' said Melchior. 'What's to stop you?'

'Come and the see the Saviour?' said Babushka. 'You shouldn't tease an old woman.'

'Why not come?' said Balthazar. 'You've nothing to keep you here.'

Babushka put her hands on her hips and laughed, though she had not laughed for many years. 'Lord bless you, there's a man talking! Nothing to keep me? Why, there's the washing and the wiping, the sweeping and the shopping, the dusting and the dishes. A person can't just get up and go on the spur of the moment – not someone like me, I mean! It's one thing for you sages and scholars, you thinkers and philosophers!' But she would have liked to go! Indeed she would! Her grey eyes shone as they had not done for many years. 'Besides, I have no present to give the Saviour.'

In the morning, the three sages said to her again, 'Come with us, Babushka! Come and see the Christ child.'

'Maybe,' she said, giving them parcels of food for the journey. 'Soon, perhaps. Maybe I'll follow on tomorrow and catch you up.'

'Don't leave it too late,' warned Melchior, as he mounted his kneeling camel.

So the three sages went on their way, and the bells on the camels' bridles jingled more and more softly as they swayed away into the distance.

Babushka cleaned her house from top to bottom. 'I will go!' she resolved. She washed her clothes for the journey.

She mended and polished her boots. 'I do have a present, after all!'

She unlocked the cupboard in the corner of the room and took out the toys which had belonged to her dead child. Then she cleaned and painted and shone and mended them all: wooden dolls and little cups, a ball, a bat, a bear. She worked all day and never noticed how the time sped by, for she liked to be busy. For a time she wept at the memory of her dead child. Then she smiled at the thought of the child newly born. How good it would be to welcome such a child into the world! How fine that the three sages thought that she – Babushka! – was a fit person to meet the Saviour of the World.

At last she packed all the toys into a basket, shut the door of her immaculate little cottage and set off after Caspar, Melchior and Balthazar. The new star in the sky had set, but it was not difficult to follow the trail of excitement and astonishment left behind by the exotic camel train.

She followed them down valleys and over hills, through villages and cities. She followed them to Jerusalem, where they had visited the palace of the Roman Governor. She followed them to Bethlehem, and rested there at an inn.

'Three wise men from foreign parts?' said the innkeeper. 'Yes, they came here, but they've gone now. So have the man and woman – and the baby, too.'

'*The baby was born here?*' asked Babushka in amazement.

'Yes, yes. In the stable. No room in here. What a night we had! Visitors, lights, singing . . . Gone now, though. You're too late.'

Into Egypt, Babushka followed the rumours of Mary and Joseph and their little baby Jesus. North, west, east and south she went on searching for the Christ child. Though her search led her nowhere, and lasted many years, she never gave up. On and on she carried her basket of toys, forgetting that the baby king must have long since grown to manhood.

Thirty years later, passing again one day by the walls of Jerusalem, she saw a terrible sight. Three men had been executed by the Romans, nailed by their hands and feet to wooden crosses on a bare hilltop, to suffer in the sun and to die. The one in the centre wore a crude twist of thorns round his head, like an imitation crown. A crowd of women stood nearby, weeping. One was the mother of the young man in the crown of thorns.

Babushka set down her heavy basket, and put her arms around the woman. 'I lost a son, too,' she said. 'My heart goes out to you.' Then she stooped to pick up her basket again.

It seemed strangely light – as if all the toys had been taken from inside. But no, when she opened the lid, they were still there, as shining and pretty as the day she packed them.

Babushka continued on her way, searching, always searching. But now she decided not to save all the toys in her basket to present to the Christ child. She would give some of them away – 'After all, every child is a child of God!' She felt sure the Christ child would understand, when at last she found him. So whenever she passed the home of a child, she left a little something by the hearth – a trumpet, a puppet, a drum.

Strange to say, her basket – though it was now as light as a feather – never emptied. Whenever she reached her hand under the lid there was still always a variety of toys at her fingertips.

She never did find whom she was looking for – or never realized that she had found him already. She is travelling still, still giving away her toys. She leaves her presents in every Christian country, in every Christian town, on every day of the year. But only on the birthday of the Christ child are her shining gifts visible to the girls and boys who wake in the half-light of morning and remember, 'It's Christmas Day!'

The Pig Goes Courting

A HAWAIIAN MYTH

H E WAS not a pretty lad. Even his mother and father blenched at their first sight of him: it was the way his snout snuffled and his ears drooped and his tusks curled right back over his ears. His manners left something to be desired, too: the way he held his bowl to his face and grunted down his food, then rooted about the floor for what he had spilled. But when it came to friendship, Kamapua'a was the man to have by you, and when it came to valour, he made the finest ally in the world. The fact that Kamapua'a had the head and body of a pig was of no importance to those who knew him. And he was a god, after all.

He lived on the island of Hawaii, where he spent most of his time frightening away invaders. There was not a foe born who did not panic and run at the sight of Kamapua'a in full charge – head down, shoulders up, tusks gleaming, and venting the most terrifying squeals. He wielded a palm tree for a club, and while he rooted about for coconuts to pitch at retreating enemies, would scoop up huge earthworks and sand dunes, the better to defend the islanders.

Sometimes, however, when Kamapua'a's mind turned from war to the finer things of life, he would trot off on his human feet, into the hills and plantations, and whistle at the pretty women swaying by. The women would laugh and cast a flirting glance, then patter home to their mothers, giggling. One day, Kamapua'a ventured further inland – to the mountainous regions – and saw a quite different breed of woman. She took away too much of his breath for him to whistle. 'Her I shall marry,' declared the pig god, gazing up at the summit where Pele stood, red hair streaming.

Pele was the fire goddess. She lived among her cantankerous relations, the volcanoes, whose grumbling could be heard all over the island. Like them, Pele had a fiery disposition (as you might expect of a fire goddess). She greeted Kamapua'a's proposal of marriage with a cackle of crackling laughter, and kicked pebbles down on his head. Then, standing on the skyline, her hands on her hips, she began to heap such invective on the pig god that his little legs bowed.

'Marry you? *You*? The nut-snuffling, trough-grubbing, bristle-backed hog of a bacon-flitch? You sugar-cane-crashing bore? You yard of lard? Who do you think you're speaking to?'

'I'm a boar, not a bore,' said Kamapua'a, grinning with delight, 'and who else in the world do you think is going to take you, you lump of hot coal, you furnace-mouth, you spark-burned hearthrug?'

Pele thumbed her nose. 'Filthy mud-rolling, rubbish eating, snout-nosed heap of brawn!'

'You collision of glow-worms! Bad-dream-on-a-hot-night! Indigestible bunch of red chillies!'

Pele spat fire, but Kamapua'a simply raised up a mound of earth to deflect it. 'Come down and take the only bridegroom who'll ever have you! Together we'll be pork and crackling!'

So they went on, hurling insults as big as coconuts, until the relations began to join in. The volcanoes trembled, and their vents poured out foul-smelling jets of yellow sulphur. Lightning jumped about excitedly, jabbing a stabbing finger at Kamapua'a and his family and using such words as burned holes in the heavens. Kamapua'a's friends rallied to him in defence of his good name.

It began to look less like a wooing than a war, as the two sides bombarded each other with aspersions and expletives. Words gave way to weapons. At first, Pele only hurled thunderbolts and fireballs, while Kamapua'a threw back cakes of mud and litter off the beach: seaweed and empty turtle shells. But the squabbling escalated.

'Go home, you ugly brute, or my aunts and uncles will erupt and drown you all in molten lava!'

'Look out, Kamapua'a,' muttered his friends uneasily. 'They could do for us if they put their minds to it.'

'Not if we call up reinforcements,' said Kamapua'a, scratching himself luxuriously against a palm tree. He turned his snout towards the sky and bellowed: *'Come clouds! Come sparkling springs, come damp dewfall and splashy sea! Come wet rain and fuming fog! Come moist mists and running rivers! Rise up and teach these volcanoes a lesson that will silence their grumbling for ever! I'll have you pleading to marry me, Pele, you see if I don't!'*

So all the moist things of the islands ganged together. Springwater leapt up and, together with streams and rills and rivers, ringed the mountains round with water. But when the cascades of orange lava spilled from the throats of Pele's ghastly relations, they dissolved the water in clouds of steam. Mountains of ash blotted out the sky, and rained down, hot and choking, on the pig god, till he stood hock-deep in cinders. But he simply blared at the clouds to do their worst, and the clouds burst over the volcanoes and drenched them in torrents of rain.

Magma seethed and bubbled. Brimstone and pumice rattled down on Kamapua'a, white-hot or dripping orange lava. But though he squealed ear-splitting yelps of rage, he also summoned up the fogs and mists that live in the morning forests. Like gigantic ghosts, they advanced on the erupting uplands, grappling and interweaving with the yellow clouds of sulphurous smoke, the plumes of steam. There was a hissing like a million angry snakes, a coughing and choking, a spluttering and sputtering. Then, one by one, like snuffed candles, the volcanic fires went out, and Pele's aunts and uncles were reduced to rumbling grumblers, chuntering and mumbling: ' . . . these disrespectful youngsters . . .'

Pele, her red hair hanging in sodden hanks, came stumbling blindly through the dense fog, feeling her way and shivering. Kamapua'a plunged forward and, before her eyes even opened, took Pele's two hands in his. 'Give in to me, Lady of Fire! The world is more water than fire: my longing for you will always be greater than your loathing. Give in. Fire and earth and air and water should work together – make something out of nothing – not reduce the world to dust and ashes! Let's join forces, you and I. I may look more pig than man, but you'll find I'm more god than either.'

She never made a quiet bedfellow. Pele's temper was forever flaring up. But her passion for Kamapua'a, once lit, was as hot as her temper. And soon, when her uncles and aunts grumbled and rumbled at the heart of the island, complaining that the world was changing. Pele would laugh as loud as Kamapua'a, and they would run down to the beach together and drink coconut milk till both their snouts were quite white.

Can Krishna Die?

AN INDIAN LEGEND

MANY GODS have visited the earth. Wherever their feet trod, myths have grown up, and wherever they lived legends are left, like fossils, in the rocks. But none of the gods has stayed long. For gods can only visit by becoming flesh and blood, and flesh and blood are vulnerable like butter in the hot sun.

When the great Lord Krishna was born to live among the cowherds and milkmaids of Yadava, however, it seemed he must live forever. He was so strong that no man or beast or monster could overpower him. He was such a warrior that no enemy could stand in his way. He was so handsome that women cherished him as a child and adored him as a grown man. He had children, and his children had children, and it seemed that Krishna must live to bless and protect his family through endless generations. Old age ran off him like rain off a raven's wing.

Then, one day, a joke went badly wrong. A band of wise men came wandering through the meadows, frail, gaunt, aged, and without one smile between them. The young cowherds of Yadava had no respect for their age and wisdom.

'Let's see if they're really so wise,' said one.

'Let's see if they even know a cow from a bull!' said another.

They called Samba, grandson of Krishna, and dressed him in women's clothes. His long hair was curly and his cheek was smooth, so that once dressed in a sari, he looked as pretty as any milkmaid. In his right hand he held a pestle for pounding rice, under his dress a cushion, and on his face a silly simper.

'O wise men! O sage scholars of a thousand learned words! Cast your clever eyes over this girl and tell us what manner of child she will have when it is born.'

Samba found it all so funny that he let slip the cushion, which fell to the ground with a thud.

The cowherds laughed till their legs gave way: they laughed till the cows took fright. But the sage old men did not laugh. Their sad rheumy eyes looked down at the cushion and at Samba's large, masculine feet.

'So you think it is funny, do you, to make fun of your elders and betters? So you have no respect for the magic of our wisdom? Then with our wisdom of magic *we curse you*!' Their yellow eyes flashed and their gnarled fingers pointed at Samba. 'May that woman's pestle of yours strike dead every young man in the tribe of Yadava!'

Laughter tailed away. The air was cold with the chill of the curse. The leaves on the trees shook.

Before the sage old men had limped out of sight, Samba had smashed the wooden pestle in two. The two halves he burned in the fire till they turned to ash, then he ground the ash into finest dust. Finally he sprinkled the dust into the sea, where it sank.

'There!' said Samba, brushing his hands together. 'How shall the pestle kill us when there is no pestle?' And every man there breathed a sigh of relief. For though they did not fear to die, their insulting joke had put in danger the life of the Lord Krishna.

Down in the dark of the deep-fathomed sea, the powdered ash settled on the sand. Like seed it took root. Like seed it sprang up. Salt sea grasses grew, as straight and brittle as reeds of glass, and in among the stems swam the bright fish of the ocean.

Amid its own bubbling cloud of silver breath, a little fish

nibbled the sea grasses, the crawling snail, the wriggling worm . . . and the silver hook inside that worm. With scarcely a struggle, the fish was pulled from the water by a fisherman, who carried it home in delight and ate it for supper with his family. No cowherd this fellow, for he loved the challenge of hunting – boar in the forest, lions in the hills, fish in the sea, and birds on the wing.

The cowherds of Yadava preferred to roast an ox, eat cheese from the creamery, and drink wine from the fruit in the orchards. Sitting on the beach at low tide, they celebrated their narrow escape, and laughed (as loud as they dared) at the thought of foiling that dreadful curse.

Everyone was there – Krishna, his brother Balarama, Samba and all the Yadava cattlemen. The sea ebbed, but the wine flowed – heavy, heady wine. The brittle reeds on the shoreline tinkled like glass chimes in the breeze. They drank in celebration – and the drink make them want to dance. The dancing made them thirsty, and so they drank some more. The drink made them thirstier – as thirsty as if they had drunk the salt sea – so they drank still more.

The ocean rolled, the drinkers reeled. The tide turned, and the mood of the drinkers turned too, from cheerfulness to surliness, from surliness to a fighting madness.

For no good reason, one pushed another. He rolled back in among the reeds and one snapped off in his hand. He threw it like a spear, and it stabbed the young man in the throat. All at once a nonsensical quarrel turned into a frenzied battle. The lads took sides, the sides took arms – they broke off the sharp reeds and hurled them, with drunken lunges, blindly at one another. Balarama was pierced in the back and the cold of the sages' curse chilled him to the marrow. 'Go. Krishna! get away!' he called. Then he dragged himself into the shade of a tree and sat patiently watching Death approach like a ship across the wide sea.

That poisonous curse cankered each graze, turned every

cut into a deadly wound. By sunset, not a cowherd was left to call the cows to milking. Every one lay dead on the beach. The milkmaids watching for returning herds waited till night settled over them, and with it a sense of dread.

Krishna alone walked from the beach, his face full of anguish, his heart full of regret. He went deep into the forest, where the light was slight and green. Only the wind through the branches sounded the same as the sea. He thought back over his life – the women he had loved, the children he had cradled, the battles he had won. He thought about the vastness between the stars, the heat within the suns, the length of history and the shortness of life. Not another soul moved through the green shade of the forest.

None, that is, but the huntsman. Today he had left his fishing rod at home and come in search of deer, with bow and arrow. His newest arrow hung at his side – the one tipped with sharpened fish bone cut from the remains of his fish dinner.

A movement, a shadow shape. A deer?

The huntsman drew back his bow and fired, and Krishna, darling of the world, buckled his leg in pain. The arrow tip had pierced the sole of his foot, and the cold curse was already coursing through his veins.

So he laid his earthly life aside. Like a snake who sloughs off the papery glory of its skin to grow the greater, Krishna sloughed off his human form and returned to Heaven – a creature of spirit, a divine being once more, a radiance like the brightness left in your eye after looking at the sun.

The Lighthouse on the Lake

A JAPANESE LEGEND

THERE was once a lighthouse-keeper, tall and slender like his lighthouse and as dazzling to women as the light he tended. His name was Jimmu, and he sat in his high tower, feeling like the sun generously bestowing its beams on Lake Biwa.

A beautiful girl, Yuki, who lived on the shores of the lake, saw him out fishing one summer's day, and fell in love, as only a young girl can. Her soul, her life, her heart, her all, she placed in her father's boat, and rowed out to Jimmu. 'I love you,' she said.

Jimmu wound in his hook and attached another worm, looking at the girl. 'Pretty little thing,' he thought, and said, 'I'm honoured. But your parents will never allow us to meet. You're so young.'

'I could row over the lake to your lighthouse after dark. My parents would never even know.'

Jimmu was taken aback. It was such a very daring suggestion! The vast lake is a pretty place on a sunny day, but at night it is an eerie crevasse of gleaming dark between the looming Hira mountains. Yuki was certainly a remarkable girl if she was ready to cross the night lake. And how shameless! To suggest such a lover's tryst with a stranger, without a word about marriage. Jimmu was almost shocked . . . but pleasantly excited too.

'Until tonight, then,' he said, and her face filled with such joy that he congratulated himself on making her so happy.

That night, Yuki slipped from her bed and crept to the

waterside. She launched her father's rowing boat and unshipped the oars. Then, fixing her course by the lighthouse's shining beacon, she rowed towards her handsome lighthouse-keeper.

In her mind, she pictured happy days ahead: marriage, children, a little house like her parents' by the lake shore, a garden in the shadow of the lighthouse . . . When the prow of the boat bumped the steps at the foot of the tall building, a smiling figure stood waiting with outstretched hand to help her ashore. She saw in Jimmu's smile everything she wanted to see: true love, a kind heart, a longing to share his whole life with her. She would help him trim the wick of his lamp, help him polish the mirrors in the lamp-room. She would cook the fish he caught in the lake each day, and bear him sons to work the lighthouse in Jimmu's old age.

Night after night, Yuki visited her lover at the Hira lighthouse. No one ever knew. She rowed through sharp frost, her breath like smoke. She rowed through driving rain, her hair stuck to her like otter's fur. She rowed through summer lightning, when jagged forks jabbed at a meat-raw sky and tore it to shreds.

Jimmu marvelled at her bravery, then he revelled in her love. He even mentioned marriage, in a vague sort of way – and almost meant it. After she was gone – rowing home before dawn could betray her secret – Jimmu would lie awake, looking at the haze of light around his lighthouse window, and wonder at his good fortune.

'She's better than any girl I ever met,' he thought one August night, as he watched her little boat approach along the golden path of light. 'Who else would do this for me? I shall marry her.' The night was windy: the waves were higher than usual, and Yuki's progress was slow.

'Although, really, she ought to show more modesty.'

The little boat pitched and Yuki's oars flailed like the legs of some water-borne insect.

'Perhaps she behaves like this with all the men – a flirt – a man-chaser!' thought Jimmu, ' . . . although when would she have time to visit anyone else?'

Yuki stopped rowing to peel the wet hair away from her eyes.

'Perhaps she's mad with love for me because I'm so desirable,' thought Jimmu. 'No one else has ever rowed across the lake to cook me dinner.' His wondering began to change to anxiety.

'Perhaps she's just mad,' thought Jimmu. 'I'd be mad myself if I married a madwoman.' Then came the worst possibility of all.

'Perhaps she's not a woman at all! Perhaps she's a demon sent to tempt me! Maybe she's an enchantress weaving an evil spell, even now, to trap me like a fly in a web! Yes! That's it! She's an evil spirit! A spirit of the lake!'

The heart which had felt so little real affection for Yuki experienced an unfamiliar pang of fright, a quiver of pure self-love. He must show the Powers of Evil that he was not a wicked man at all – no, not at all! He could resist temptation! He had no need of ghostly temptresses! The thought of Yuki's arms round his neck made him shiver with horror, now that his foolish imagination had convinced him she was a dream.

Leaping up the stairs to the lamp-room, he shielded his eyes against the brightness of the burning tallow wick and its mirrored reflections. His own shadow danced hugely against the wall. Jimmu snuffed out the flame with a leather bag, and coughed himself breathless in the acrid smoke.

Out on the lake, Yuki was plunged into total darkness. The golden path of light along which she had been rowing drowned in an instant, and left her blind. Gradually her eyes made out her own pale hands on the oars, the wet oars themselves, but beyond her oar's end, nothing – blackness.

She was instantly disorientated. 'Jimmu! Dearest! The

light! The light has gone out! Jimmu! Trim the wick! I can't see the lighthouse! I can't see the shore!'

The darkness fell on her like slurry, stopping up her eyes and ears and nose and mouth. 'Jimmu!' she tried to call, but the wind tore the words from her lips and repaid them with spray. One oar pulled free of its rowlock and drifted away from the boat. 'Jimmu, help me! Shine a light! Call out to me! It's your own little Yuki! Why don't you hear me? Help me. Jimmu! I'm lost!'

In the lamp-room of the lighthouse, Jimmu sat with his hands over his ears, telling himself, 'A demon would say anything to trick a man out of his soul!' He refused to hear. He shut his eyes and ears, and put out the flame of love in his heart as assuredly as he had snuffed out the wick.

Yuki went on calling. Though her little boat was filling with rain, though she had spun and drifted far out into the centre of the lake, still she went on calling: 'In the name of everything we mean to each other, light the light, Jimmu!'

When the second oar broke loose, she tried to retrieve it, leaning out too far. The boat capsized, and Yuki was plunged face-first into the icy black waves. As the cold soaked through her clothes, so the realization crept into her soul.

Jimmu had betrayed her. She saw, with terrible clarity, all that she had been too dazzled to see by lamplight: that Jimmu did not love her at all, had never loved her, cared nothing for her fate. She pulled herself carefully across the upturned boat, straddling the slimy keel.

'I curse you, Jimmu. Do you hear me now? I curse your lighthouse, and I curse you! I curse this lake which carried me to you, and I curse the mountains which looked on and did nothing to stop me! Disaster fall on you as it fell on me the day I saw Jimmu the lighthouse-keeper!' Then she let go her grip on the keel, and allowed herself to slide into the heaving lake, dropping like the lead on a fish-line directly to the bottom.

A jag of wind caught the empty boat and rolled it across the lake, smashing it against the base of the lighthouse. Another roused the waves to riot, foam crests seething into sudden life, ripping the crayfish pots from their tethers. The wind redoubled, pulling slates off the roof of Yuki's little house, and branches off the shoreside trees. Out from behind the mountains came a twist of wind more ferocious than bears or mounted swordsmen. It raced across the lake, wrenching into the sky a million gallons of angry water.

The hurricane struck the lighthouse with wind and water, rubble and fish, wreckage and tree trunks and birds. It crazed the lamp-room like an eggshell, and tore the mortar from between the bricks. Trapped inside, Jimmu glimpsed the night sky through a hundred opening cracks. A moment later, the floor collapsed, and dropped him the height of the lighthouse as if down a deep, dark well.

Next day, nothing remained of the lighthouse on the shores of Lake Biwa. And now, each August, hurricanes spring from behind the mountains and lash the lake into a maelstrom, destroying, uprooting, demolishing the calm remains of summer. They come as regularly as a lover keeping a tryst with her sweetheart, but their twisting embrace is deadly and, at heart, a whirling emptiness.

King Arthur Gives Back
his Sword

A CELTIC LEGEND

LEGEND speaks of a king who ruled when the world had need of heroes, and taught men the nature of chivalry. His name was Arthur Pendragon and his kingdom was in the west. There was druid magic in his hands – a pure, white magic that gave him the strength to strike and the authority to govern. He carried the great sword Excalibur and, by his side, its magic scabbard which protects the wearer from wounds.

He gathered around him a family of knights – good men (or well-intentioned, at least) – and made them swear to seek adventure and fight evil wherever they found it. To teach them humility, he seated them at a round table, giving no one pride of place, not even himself.

But knights are by nature competitive. They are trained from boyhood to win in the joust, to win in battle, to prove themselves the best. Equality and accord are not in the nature of knights. So inevitably rivalries, jealousies, petty differences broke out, which grew into feuds. The company of the Round Table began to split and splinter like a wheel embedded in a rut.

Open rebellion arose at last, led by Mordred, who drew to his side an army big and cruel enough to trample down a legion of angels. Arthur and his faithful knights prepared to fight the last great battle. They were hugely outnumbered, but by a rabble so grubbing, greedy and unremarkable that they amounted to mere brass pennies – dozens needed to equal one silver knight.

Between tents fringed with blood, from daisy-eyed morning to sunflower noon, the two armies fought – cavalry charges like crashing surf, axes hammering out on shields the great drumbeat of war. The dark rabble of Mordred's infantry fell away, but the shining company of Arthur shrank, too. At last, only the black knight-champions of Mordred remained, and fought in single combat with the knights of the Round Table. Man by man they died, not one falling without his opponent paying the same price.

Finally, Arthur and Mordred met in the shadow of a castle wall and a cry went up that silenced the rooks in the treetops. 'All day I have pursued you, Mordred, and you have kept shifting ground. Are you afraid of dying or of damning your soul with treason by fighting your lawful king?'

'I am afraid of nothing,' said Mordred, and the word 'nothing' was in his mouth when Arthur's lance struck him a blow which shattered his armour like the ice on a lake. Looking down at the gaping wound in his chest, Mordred drew back his lips in a snarl. He pushed forward along the lance – as a boar will sometimes thrust on to the hunter's spear – and wielding his broadsword one last time, struck Arthur a blow that cracked his breastplate. 'Die, Arthur Pendragon! Die and be forgotten!'

Impaled on the royal lance, Mordred died on his knees. Arthur fell backwards into the arms of Sir Bedivere. 'Where are my other knights?'

'I am all that is left, sire.'

'What, only one? It is enough,' whispered Arthur. 'It takes only one man to tell the world: this is how it was, this is how it ended . . . Lift me up.'

'I'll fetch a stretcher – the women of the castle will help

me carry you indoors. You can rest there. Get better . . .'
said Bedivere.

'No. My time has come. Lift me on your back and carry
me into that wood over there.' The magic in Arthur's eyes
could still command Bedivere's obedience. As Bedivere
carried him, Arthur spoke despite his pain. 'I have been
here once before. When I was newly crowned, Merlin the
Magician brought me here – to the shore of a lake in the
middle of the forest. It was here that I was given Excalibur.
It is entrusted to earthly kings only once in a thousand
years, you know. It made me what I am.'

'Your goodness and God's help made you that, my liege,'
said Bedivere, feeling tears cold on his cheeks.

'A witch stole the scabbard, or Mordred could not have
wounded me today. But every man must die, Bedivere.
Every man deserves to rest.'

It grew dark, but still Bedivere plodded on through the
wood, along a baffling maze of paths, carrying Arthur
across his shoulders. Suddenly, a lake lay in front of him –
an eye of light, mirroring the moon. Bedivere lay Arthur
Pendragon down between the roots of an oak tree.

'I haven't the strength, Bedivere. Please – as a last act of
friendship – return Excalibur to the lake for me . . .'

'Throw it in, you mean?' Sir Bedivere took the grand
sword from Arthur's hip. He was exhausted himself and
could barely carry it. It seemed a terrible waste of a sword,
an ignoble and obscure end for the mighty Excalibur. So
before he got to the lake, he hid the sword under some
bracken and turned back towards his master.

'What did you see?' asked the King, pulling himself
upright.

'See? Well, I . . . er . . . I saw the ripple stir the reeds,
and moorhens hurrying away . . .'

'Liar!' said Arthur in a voice that turned Bedivere's
blood to water. 'Go back and do as I said!'

Bedivere turned and ran back to the sword. He *did* mean

to throw it, he did almost throw it: twice he whirled it round his head. But then he thought of his task: to preserve the legend of Arthur and his knights, and keep the wonder and faith alive in the hearts of the people. How much easier it would be if he kept Excalibur for the world to see!

So he laid the sword down again on a cushion of moss, and went back to Arthur.

'What did you see?' asked the King.

'I saw a skein of geese and a shoal of fishes rise in a cloud of bubbles . . .'

'Traitor! Villain!' cried Arthur in a voice which turned Bedivere's blood to gall. Clutching the tree, trying to get up, he demanded. 'Must I do it myself, after all?'

'No! No! I'll do it! I will!' Back through the trees Bedivere ran, in a frenzy of regret, thinking that the last words his king spoke to him would be in reproach. He snatched up the great sword, swung it three times round his head, staggering deep into the lake under the huge weight. Then he let it go, and it whirled about and about, a fragment of lightning, a sliver of moon.

In the centre of the lake, just where the moon's reflection floated like a pallid face, an arm clad in white silk reached out of the water – a woman's arm, a woman's hand, but with strength enough to catch Excalibur by its hilt, brandish it three times and draw it down into the lake.

Bedivere went back and told the King what he had seen. It seemed to pacify Arthur, to free him of his anxiety. A smile came to his lips, but he could barely speak any longer.

Suddenly, Bedivere heard behind him the splash of oars and ran to the waterside, thinking perhaps to glimpse the Lady of the Lake bearing Excalibur. But what he saw was a long, slender barge being rowed towards him by three veiled women in tissue-fine robes of grey. They beached the boat and moved ashore past Bedivere, lifting the King to his feet and leading him the short way to their craft. It seemed an easy journey for him, like a man walking to his own bed after a day's hard labour.

Just when Bedivere thought he was dreaming, the women spoke to him. 'We are taking your lord to Avalon.'

'Where he may rest and sleep and recover from the wounds of life.'

'Do not mourn for him.'

'How can I help but mourn?' said Bedivere. 'The world will be lost without him.'

'If there is ever a danger of the world being lost, young man,' said the tallest of the women, 'Arthur will come again, armed with the sword Excalibur. But for now, the world is not lost. Indeed, you saw it saved today from the forces of Evil. Don't forget that when you tell the history of Arthur, when you recount the legend of the Round Table.'

The barge floated out from the shore, two women at the oars, the third cradling the King's head in her lap. He seemed to be asleep now, at rest, and the barge moved silently out across the lake, to be swallowed up by scarves of mist, curtains of diaphanous moonlight, hangings of velvet night.

A Bloodthirsty Tale

I T IS A story told all over the world. The Creator makes Humankind. Humankind disappoint their Creator. The Creator destroys what he has made. So it was with Re, in the days when he ruled both the world of people on Earth as well as the family of gods in Heaven.

'People are hatching plots against me! They are rebellious and disobedient. I don't know why I ever created them or any of their kind!' complained Re. 'And yet . . .'

And yet Re was fond of his creation, and did not want to wipe people altogether off the face of the Earth. A small punishment would serve, perhaps, to put the humans in their proper place, to teach them a lesson in humility.

So Re took the third eye from his forehead – the one which shone so brightly, as he sailed the Ship-of-a-Million-Days across Heaven – his eye, the Sun.

When Re wished (as now he wished), his eye took on the shape of a goddess, Hathor. Generally, Hathor was gentle and kind, but since the eye had bulged with fury as Re took it from his head, this time Hathor too was filled with furious rage. Snatching up a sword, she rushed out into the deserts, herding and chasing crowds of people ahead of her like flocks of frightened sheep. She laid about them with teeth and blade, killing and rending, till the human race cried aloud for the gods to pity them.

Only sunset put an end to the slaughter, when Hathor reported to Re in the Ship-of-a-Million-Days and was congratulated for her good work. Re reached out a hand to turn her back into his eye. 'Return to me. O Powerful One. This day shall be remembered for ever in the history of the world!'

But Hathor stepped out of reach. 'Tomorrow I shall kill the rest!' she declared, laughing wildly. 'The sands of the desert will turn red with their blood!' Her hands dripped blood, and she smeared it across her cheeks and hair like warpaint. 'When I have finished my work the history of people on Earth will be at an end! I have tasted their blood and I mean to drink every last drop!'

Re shuddered. 'I've never seen her like this. She means to kill them all!' he realized with a pang of sorrow. He had not meant things to go so far. The people of Earth were, after all, the flowers he had planted for a garden: he did not want them scythed down to the last bright petal.

'Quick!' he told his messengers. 'Go to the Island of Elephantine, in the centre of the Nile, and fetch me its bright red soil!' Crocodiles plunged into the river; cranes flew upstream. There, in the river, as scarlet as the back of the swimming hippopotamus god, lay the island of Elephantine, rich in red ochre. It was smaller by half, after the messengers of Re had scoured away its soil.

'Quick! Quick!' Re told the High Priest of the temple at Memphis. 'Pound this red earth to dust!'

'Quick! Quick! Quick!' he told the servant girls who worked in the fields. 'Brew beer and ferment it with honey!'

All night, the priests pounded and the girls brewed. Then, just before dawn, Re took the dusty dye and seven thousand pints of foaming beer, and mixed the two together till they thickened and congealed into a gleaming red liquor.

One jug at a time, Re poured out the thick red beer on to the ground. Seven thousand jugs of oozing redness he poured out, until he and the priests and the serving girls stood ankle deep in it.

Then he sailed away in the Ship-of-a-Million-Days, as though the fate of the human race were of no concern to him.

Hathor, the eye of Re, woke from her slumbers and remembered her task for the day. She lifted her bloody sword and strode out into the world of people.

Splash, splash, splash, her feet waded into a lake of red. She looked around her and saw, as far as the eye could see, a quaggy mire of gore. 'Indeed, I am the glory of Re that I spilled so much blood in a single day!' And in her blood-lust, she knelt down and drank what she mistook for the blood of Humankind.

She had not remembered it tasting so good! 'If this is how the blood of my enemy tastes, then I shall kill and drink and drink and kill till the last mewling baby has paid for angering my master! Where are they hiding themselves? Let me root them out, these wretches! I, Hathor, am their doom!'

But after drinking a thousand jugs of the blood-red liquor, Hathor found she could not readily get to her feet to go after the remainder of Humankind. She could only manage to sit, with her feet dangling in the red lake, and drink a thousand jugs more.

Soon after, an unaccountable desire to sleep came over Hathor. She squinted up at the Ship-of-a-Million-Days, bearing the gods on high, but it seemed to be spinning about like an angry bluebottle. She watched it for as long as her eyes would stay open, then fell backwards with a splash into the deepest, darkest drunken stupor the world has ever seen.

'Oooh, my head! Oh, my bursting head! Almighty Re, take pity on your servant! I'm not well!' When Hathor woke from her beery dreams, she could remember nothing about the day before. 'How did I get here? What am I doing here?

Where is the comfortable forehead of my master. Re? . . .
And why do I feel so *ill*?'

Re helped her to her feet, cupped her affectionately in his
hands and changed her back into his third eye, settling her
in his forehead. Though she was very bloodshot for a
while, and glowed less brightly, she was once again a
solemn and sober eye who looked down kindly on the
people of Earth.

So too did Re, for having seen them come so close to
destruction, he had learned to value them as among his best
works of creation.

Rip Van Winkle

AN AMERICAN LEGEND

'**W**ELL? You gonna feed the chickens, or what? D'you think that cow's gonna milk herself? S'pose you think sweeping the yard's beneath you! Mother told me it would be this way: me slaving my fingers to the bone and you laying up in bed, thinking you're the King of England!'

Rip Van Winkle rolled out of bed, but still his wife came after him, her bony hand pecking him through his night-shirt. It was five in the morning and today was turning out just like yesterday.

'And chop some wood if you're not too high and mighty! And mend that busted step before I fall down and kill myself. You'd like that, wouldn't you? Then you could drink alcohol and play skittles with those cheap friends of yours . . . And talking of that – I've told you till I'm blue – keep that flea-bitten dog of yours out the house, will yuh? Mother told me it would be this way: marriage.'

Rip wished *his* mother had told him. He wished she had led him aside on his wedding day and said, 'You don't want to do this, son. Here's a gun: go shoot yourself instead.'

He got dressed, swept the yard, chopped wood, fed the chickens and milked the cows. He cooked breakfast for his wife, picked the dog hairs off the rug, and made the beds. It was still only six o'clock and the day lay ahead of him like a pile of rocks.

As he mended the fence, his work took him farther and farther away from the house. The shouting grew fainter and fainter. ' . . . *and you let those slugs get to the cabbages again!*' Rip suddenly thought that if he walked way up the hill, he would not be able to hear it at all. His dog Bark looked at him, harassed and hangdog. 'Let's go,' said Rip. And they did.

He knew there would be heck to pay when he got home, but as he climbed between the red pine and maple trees, and breathed the scent of the ferns, Rip hardly cared. He walked and walked up the gorge, deep into the canyon, where the sound of falling water scrawls out every other sound. 'Hear that, Bark? Peace. Perfect peace,' he said.

Up past Sentry Bridge, Minnehaha Falls and Frowning Cliff he climbed, where the sunlight barely trickled through the oaks but the stream plummeted down like silver mercury. And when he reached Rainbow Falls he sat down among the plaited colours of spray. He had never been so far up the glen before. Even his dog sat so still that white-tailed deer and stripy raccoons strolled by, unconcerned, and a chipmunk rolled among the moccasin flowers. At least, Rip thought it was a chipmunk at first.

Then he looked again and saw the hat, the clothes and little boots. And the barrel.

'Dang, blam and fliminy bosh!' cursed the dwarf, as the barrel he had been pushing rolled away from him towards the brink of the falls. He pulled his hat right down, so as not to see it go.

Rip Van Winkle took two big strides and stopped the barrel with his foot. 'Can I carry this some place for you?'

The dwarf pulled his hat off again and peered upwards. 'That's mighty neighbourly, sir, coming from a giant. My back's plumb busted trying to get it up the hill.'

He led the way up a staircase of slippery black stones which led right behind the Rainbow Falls. Half expecting to be washed away, Rip followed with the barrel, and Bark kept close to his heels. Behind the thunder of the waterfall, they found a little door, and behind the door, a great tavern

– a cavern of a tavern, noisy with fifty or sixty dwarfs. By getting down on his hands and knees, Rip could just squeeze in through the door. Once inside, there was room for him to stand. At the sight of Rip, the dwarfs stopped stock-still and stared.

'He helped me with the keg!' explained the first dwarf.

'Swell, but who is he?'

'What's he doing hereabouts?'

'Maybe he's dwarf-hunting.' Their voices echoed round the cave and, when Bark trotted in, they cowered against the far wall.

'I'm Rip Van Winkle, and I'm . . . well, I'm hiding from my wife.' (To his relief, there were no women dwarfs in sight.)

The dwarfs let out a single groan. 'Oh, give the man a chair! Pour him a drink! Make room for the unfortunate fellow! Don't we know how it goes! *Chop the wood! Hunt a rabbit! Fetch up the stores.* Set that barrel down Rip, and make yourself at home!'

Rip grinned shyly. 'I'd better be getting back. She'll skin me alive if I don't do some chores.'

But they all rushed at him, and slapped him on the bottom (because they could not reach his back) and hugged his legs, and tugged at his fingers. 'Come and play skittles! You can be on our team!'

'That's not fair! We want him on our team!'

'You can have his dog on your team!'

'And you can have this mug of beer over your head!'

They squabbled and wrestled and giggled throughout the game. And though they lost three balls and broke a flower vase, nobody minded. Time and again, the little men helped themselves to ale from the barrel Rip had carried. 'Have a cannikin yourself!' they kept saying, but Rip only ducked his head and said shyly, 'Better not. The wife doesn't like me to touch strong drink.'

At last, cheered on by his team, Rip scattered the skittles

to the four corners of the cavern and five toppled out of the door and over the waterfall.

'We win! We win! Our team wins! Bring the hero a drink!'

It was true, the game had given him a powerful thirst. The tankards were tiny; it couldn't hurt to sip just a thimbleful of ale . . . The dwarfs set down a saucerful for Bark the dog, as well.

At the first swallow, the cavern began to spin. At the second, everyone seemed to be standing on their heads. At the third, Bark seemed to be yawning and turning pink. Then darkness closed in on Rip Van Winkle from all sides.

'Of course. Human. We should have known.'

' . . . not used to fairy beer . . .'

' . . . too strong for him,' said voices out of the darkness.

Then Rip fell asleep, and slept deeper than he had done ever since the day he first shared his big feather bed.

When he woke, there was no sign of the dwarfs. Bark's coat was remarkably dusty, but he woke when Rip patted him. Together they ducked out of the cave. The waterfall was tumbling just as before, the spray still spanning the gorge with rainbows, the white-tailed deer still grazing.

'Now we're for it,' said Rip to his dog, as they tripped up the porch. 'Better mend that step this afternoon, I guess.'

'Who are you?' said the woman at the door.

Rip was almost too startled to speak. 'You're not my wife.'

'George! There's some old-fashioned hobo at the door, says I'm not his wife. George!'

'But I . . . I . . . I live here!'

'George! Says he lives here! You wanna fetch your gun?'

'But I . . . Where's Mrs Van Winkle?'

'Never heard of her. You got the wrong address.'

'Sure you've heard of her, Mary,' said the man who came out with his gun. 'She was the old lady lived here before us.

Husband disappeared. Lived here all alone. Fell down the step and broke her neck – she was old, mind.'

Rip Van Winkle fell back a step or two. These people were not lying. The cow in the yard was not his cow. The axe on the woodpile was not his axe. Bark whimpered at the unfamiliar smells. 'Disappeared, you say? Rip Van Winkle disappeared?'

The woman on the porch scratched her head. 'Sure. Now George calls it back to my mind . . . disappeared 'bout fifty years back. Walked off one day into Watkins Glen, they say, and never came back. Folks said the fairies took him, but then folks would. Fell in the stream and drowned hisself, more like.'

Now you might think that losing your farm, losing your feather bed, losing fifty years – and all in one day – might make a man a little bleak, unsettled and resentful. But no. That was not the way it struck Rip Van Winkle. Rip Van Winkle could see a good side to most things. From the gate of his no-longer home, he walked directly into town with his dog, sat down at the bar of the saloon, and told his story to anyone who would listen.

Within a fortnight, he was the toast of Finger Lake County.

The Raven and the Moon

AN INUIT MYTH

O NCE, when the night was too dark to bear, the fishing people of the north longed for some relief from the solid black sky and its cold hail of stars. What they did not realize was that a moon had been made for the hours of darkness, just as the Sun had been made for day. But a miserly old man and his miserly young daughter, wanting to keep it for their own, locked it away with their other treasures.

Now Raven, like the magpie, likes shiny things – stones, bones, buttons and the like – and when he heard the two whispering one day about their secret hoard, he set his heart on having something out of that chest for his own collection of pretties.

There was no chance that Loona would ever marry: her father gave away nothing that was his, and Loona would never by choice leave the cottage with its chest full of valuables. So instead of courting her, Raven, with a beat of his black wings, changed himself into two wing-shaped green leaves drooping from the bough of a waterside tree. When Loona came and sat on the bank to fish, the bough brushed her face, and the leaves fluttered in at her mouth. She did not spit them out; they slipped easily down her throat and turned to a baby in her womb.

It was a little startling to find herself pregnant, but as she pointed out to her father, 'Having a baby is like getting something for nothing.'

Her old father agreed. 'And now I need never share our pretties with any son-in-law.'

So they made a crib out of furs, on rockers of whalebone, and when the child was born, laid it in the cradle. They called it Beaky, poor mite, because of its enormous hooked nose.

Beaky started to cry.

'Perhaps it's hungry,' said Loona, and fed it. But still the baby cried.

'Perhaps it's wet,' said her father, and turned over the furs in the cot. But still the baby cried.

'Perhaps it's cutting teeth,' said Loona, and gave it her forefinger to mumble on. 'Ouch! What a bite!' But still the baby cried.

'Perhaps it's sick,' said the old man, and they took turns to walk the baby up and down, up and down, up and down. But still it cried.

'Perhaps it's bored,' said Loona. 'It must have a toy to play with.' So she made it a toy horse and a toy fish and sewed it a ball out of felt. But still the baby cried.

The old miser sank his head in his hands and his fingers in his ears. He needed his sleep. He longed for peace and quiet. But his home was full of bawling, the cries so piercing, so loud, that they seemed to lift the roof and split the plank walls of the hut. They took the baby outside and showed it the lap-lap of the sea and the big skuas circling. Beaky only hid its head under Loona's clothes and howled.

'We could always show it the Moon,' said the old man, his hair quite grey and his forehead puckered with misery. Loona thought for a moment and nodded.

Together they bolted the door, hung rugs over the windows and dragged the chest into the centre of the room. Loona scraped at the dirty floor and unearthed a large key. With it she unlocked the chest. Inside was another chest and inside that was a large square box.

Inside the box was a wicker basket like a lobster pot and inside the basket was a box shaped like a tube.

Inside the tube was a leather bag and inside the leather bag was a sack.

Inside the sack was a bucket, and inside the bucket was a wooden pyramid.

Inside the pyramid was a smaller vellum container studded with stars. (Their shine was reflected in the heady black eyes of the watching baby.)

Inside the star-box was a bundle of orange cloth and, shining through the cloth, a light so bright that all shadows were banished from the room. When Loona unwrapped the cloth, out across the floor rolled a glorious silver ball shining more brightly than any coin, brighter than any flame, brighter even than the stars.

At last, to their immense relief, the baby stopped crying. It clambered out of its crib, crawled across the floor and reached out for the . . .

Loona picked up the Moon and threw it in the air playfully to make Beaky laugh. 'Higher! Higher!' chortled the baby.

The old man threw the shining ball higher still – almost as high as the smoke-hole in the centre of the ceiling. 'Higher! Higher!' cooed the baby and flailed its little arms with joy.

Loona tossed the Moon higher still, and all eyes were on the glittering treasure. So no one saw at what particular moment Raven recovered his true shape, put on black feathers and blacker beak, hunched his wings and scrabbled his claws among the ashes of the hearth.

Suddenly he sprang into the air, seized the Moon in his beak and flew with it once round the room, while Loona and her father chased him with outstretched hands. Then, with a flutter and a short cough amidst the smoke, Raven disappeared through the smoke-hole and into the night sky, carrying the Moon in his gaping beak.

Beneath him, the night shoreline was lit by moonlight for the first time. The wave tips turned to silver, the stones on the beach glimmered, the fish scales scattered along the wharf glittered. Phosphorescent algae glowed in the rock-pools.

Raven, greedy to add all these pretties to his collection, let go of the Moon which, instead of falling to earth, remained floating in the sky, out of reach of Loona, her father or anyone else. It floated too high, at last, for even the circling skuas, though some greedy beak must surely slash away at its prettiness every month, for something pares the Moon down to the tiniest sliver. Then, just when it seems to have been carried away entirely to some treasure-trove nest in the sky, there it is again, healing, growing, waxing big and white and beautiful.

Sir Patrick Spens

A SCOTS LEGEND

ALEXANDER, King of Scotland, sat in Dunfermline Town, drinking blood-red wine. His chair stood at the heart of a firelit room, the room at the heart of a castle. The rain outside could never wet the King's hair. The wind beat in vain against the castle walls. The courtiers loosened the fastenings of their velvet jackets and revelled in the warmth, the food, the dancing.

'Where are the men who will sail me a ship to Norway?' the King said.

'At this time of year, your majesty?'

'Why not? What's a little weather to one of *my* ships? I have betrothed my daughter Margaret to the Prince of Norway. But who shall have the honour of taking her to her marriage?'

An old knight sitting beside the King, half-asleep and remembering summer days, mumbled, 'Well, of course, Sir Patrick Spens is the best sea captain in all Scotland.' So the King wrote a letter commanding Sir Patrick to set sail the next day.

When the letter reached him he was walking on the beach, his grey hair tangled with the salt wind. As he read, he laughed out loud. 'Is this a joke? No one puts to sea at this time of year!'

The King's messenger neither answered nor looked him in the eye. Then Spens knew that the letter was in earnest. Deathly pale, the letter crumpling in his hand, he turned back towards the harbour. The grey sea wall curved like a beckoning arm.

He thrust his head in at the lighted door of the inn and bellowed for his crew. 'Make ready the King's ship! Men to the rigging! Men to the sheets! We sail today for Norway with the King's daughter for cargo!'

His first mate pursued him out into the cold and caught him by the sleeve. 'You don't mean it, Captain! You'll never sail today! Last night the new moon held the old in her crescent: there'll be a storm before noon, or I never read the weather in a sailor's sky!'

Spens narrowed his eyes and looked out to sea, as if he could read more than the weather in the cursive waves. 'I saw it too, old friend, but the King's command is our duty.'

A crowd of rowdy courtiers tripped and trotted down the jetty, holding on to their hats and hinnying excitedly. They thought it would be jolly to accompany the Princess Margaret. 'Oh, look now!' said one, mincing up the gangplank. 'I've wetted my new cork-heeled shoes!' Bright silk handkerchiefs fluttered on the jetty, as ladies waved goodbye to their pretty beaux.

It was only a short voyage. They reached Norway in safety, and delivered the Princess up to strangers and foreigners. Then Sir Patrick Spens and his cargo of courtiers turned back for Scotland.

At that time of year, storms prowl the Firth of Forth like winter wolves, seeking ships to devour. Only a short voyage, but the longest any man ever makes. The wind plucked off the sails like petals from a flower, and broke the mast like a green stalk. Waves rose up as high as the walls of Dunfermline Castle, and fell on the ship like stone. Out of the noise and frenzy of the storm they sailed, down, down into green silence, down, down into black cold, down, down to where the weed beckons and the fishes kiss.

That new moon has waxed and waned many times

since the ladies waved goodbye to their beaux. But come moon, go moon, they will never meet again. For the courtiers are at the bottom of the sea, ranged at the feet of Scotland's finest sea captain. Only their cork-heeled shoes and fine-feathered hats float like sea birds on the sea's shining swell.

The Saltcellar

A SCANDINAVIAN MYTH

IN THE days when the sea was sweet (though the people round it were no sweeter than now), the King of Denmark visited the King of Sweden.

'Denmark salutes you!' said King Frodi. 'May you live a thousand years!'

'Thank you,' said King Fiolnir. 'Sweden welcomes King Frodi. May your fame fill the ear of the world as the sea fills a seashell . . . Now, let's eat, and you can tell me why you've come.'

King Frodi and King Fiolnir linked arms and walked in to dinner. All through the meal, Frodi eyes the two girls who brought him his food – big, strapping Swedish girls with plaits as long as bell-ropes and muscles like bell-ringers. 'I hear they pull men like wishbones,' he said wistfully, to King Fiolnir.

'Were you looking for a wife, perhaps?' asked Fiolnir politely.

'Good heavens, no! We have plenty of *pretty* women in Denmark. No, I'm looking for two strong sla . . . workers,' said Frodi mysteriously. 'I have . . . I have some work that needs doing.'

'Then you shall have Fenia and Menia!' declared King Fiolnir. He would be sorry to lose the girls, but hospitality demanded he should give his visitor what he most desired.

Fenia and Menia were women you could moor a boat to with an easy mind. Their knees were as big as capstans and their plaits hung like ships' hawsers past shoulders like harbour moles. They were jolly, willing workers, too. King Frodi accepted them eagerly and took them home – the prize he had sought far and wide.

For at home in Denmark, King Frodi had a mill, and now he had someone to turn it.

The mill had been given him by the King of Giants, two round stones balanced one on the other like twin pillows of rock. But they were so huge that no one in all Denmark had been able to move the grindstones round. What a reward awaited Frodi, now that Fenia and Menia could make the stones turn! For it was a magic mill: from between its bulging lips poured whatever was asked of it.

Frodi asked for gold, and the girls turned the treadwheel, and the mill ground gold dust.

Frodi asked for peace, and the girls turned the tread-wheel, and the mill ground peace.

Frodi asked for happiness for all of Denmark. But he never gave a thought to Fenia and Menia, who turned the magic mill. He chained them to the treadwheel, and day and night they worked.

'When may we rest?' asked the millers, toiling round their wheel.

'When the cuckoo stops singing,' said Frodi, feeling the gold dust run through his fingers.

'But the cuckoo sings day and night. When may we sleep?' asked the giant millers, walking their wheel.

'Only while you are singing,' said Frodi, and laughed to see the barrels filling up with peace.

Fenia and Menia could not sleep while they sang, as Frodi well knew, but then Frodi did not know that they could sing at all. He certainly did not know that Fenia and Menia could sing magic songs. 'Sleep while you're singing,' said Frodi unkindly, so the sisters began to sing a song in their own mellifluous language:

'Come some army with millions of horses;
Come some army with myriads of men;
Come some fleet with battalions of pirates,
And kill this king who has chained us here!

Come you foes of dirty Denmark;
Come you foes of Frodi King.
Come you foes of peace and prosperity,
And kill this man who has made us slaves!'

That very night, despite the reefs of peace piled round Frodi's palace, pirates came raging up the rocky shore. A sea-king called Mysing and an army of mermen killed Frodi in his treasure-house, and left him headdown in a barrel of peace.

They stole the mill and they stole its millers. They stole the treadwheel and they stole the gold. They carried them all on to their flagship and put out to sea before Denmark even woke.

'Welcome aboard, sweet maidens!' said Mysing, smiling.

'You have set us free!' said Fenia. 'We can breathe again!'

'We can see the sky,' said Menia, 'and feel the starlight running down our hair!' And they danced on deck as the ship crossed the bar.

'Grind, sweet maidens,' said Mysing, smiling.

'For our rescuers? Anything! Name it!' said the girls.

'Grind me out *salt*,' said Mysing, smiling. 'Fine white salt, more precious than gold. For I am a salt merchant and sell rare salt to the kings of the world, to flavour their royal meat.'

'Fine white salt for the sea-king Mysing!' sang Fenia and Menia, skipping round their wheel. 'Fine white salt for the tables of royalty!' and the salt poured down into the holds below.

On and on till midnight Fenia and Menia trotted round

the treadwheel, grinding. The moon rose up as white as salt and the Dog Star licked it. Then the ship's brass bell rang midnight.

'Time to rest,' said Fenia and Menia. 'More salt tomorrow, but now we are sleepy.'

'Grind more salt!' said Mysing, and lashed shut the door with anchor chains. 'You'll stop when I say, and not before!'

Fenia looked at Menia. Life had not been fair. Workers in Sweden, slaves in Denmark, and now captives even on the sweet free-running sea. 'Let's grind our salt, then,' they said to each other. 'Enough and more than our dear master Mysing wants.'

They ground out salt till the holds were full.

Then they ground out more, even when Mysing thanked them and asked them to stop.

They ground out salt while the crew was sleeping, and they ground out salt till the sun came up. The sun lit a ship blizzard-white with salt. Mounds rounded the decks, dunes buried the bridge, and the ship wallowed as low as a basking whale.

'Stop! Stop! *Stop!* screamed Mysing for the thousandth time, ladling salt overboard with his two hands. But Fenia and Menia went on working.

Still the salt poured from the magic mill, stifling the mermen in their hammocks. Still Fenia and Menia skipped round their treadwheel, making more salt than ever Mysing had carried over the sea.

At last, with a groan, the overladen ship dipped its prow beneath the waves. Mysing, who was halfway up the mast, climbing up towards the sky, saw his precious cargo of salt turn transparent under the first green flood. Then his ship fell away from under him, into the deep sweet ocean.

The might of the sea and the strong sea tides are still turning the magic mill. Like a prayer wheel it revolves in the sea's dark cellars making salt. If it had been grinding peace when the ship sank, there might be fewer wars. If it had been grinding gold, then sailors would all be as rich as emperors. But the mill was grinding salt when it sank to the sea's cellars and it has ground out salt now for a thousand years and more.

That is why the seas are salty and all salt merchants poor. None is poorer than Mysing, however, who lies trapped beneath the millstones, his bones ground down and his soul salt-corroded away.

As for Fenia and Menia, they escaped from the tread-wheel as it rolled along the sea bed, struck out for the surface and swam for home. Their knees were like capstans and their plaits ships' hawsers, and their shoulders as big as harbour moles. So it may well be that they reached dry land, where they pulled more men like wishbones, or sang magic songs, and savoured the salty starlight running down their golden hair.

The Bronze Cauldron

A WELSH LEGEND

THREE paces from the door, three paces from the window, three paces from where Boy Gwion slept on the floor, stood the witch's bronze cauldron on three bronze legs. It was always bubbling, always steaming, filling the room with horrible smells. Boy Gwion had to gather twigs to feed the fire under it. He had to weed the garden, feed the dogs, sweep the floor, bake the bread, and wash the clothes – though the Old White Sow never changed hers. No one dared come near the witch's house, so Boy's life was lonely. But he was not one to complain.

In the next room, Afagddu the witch's son slept in a white bed and never went hungry. But Boy would not have changed places with Afagddu. His face was as ugly as a dish of eels, and the rest of him all clenched up like a fist. He was the reason why the Old White Sow came and went, to and fro, day and night, feeding the great bronze cauldron.

She brought things soft and hard, blue things and red, nameless things and things too horrible to name. Sometimes she took a ladle and poured a drop of the brew down Afagddu's throat. But he only gaped back at her like a cuckoo chick, his two eyes dull as mud. 'Not yet, not yet,' crooned the Old White Sow kissing his scurvy head, 'but one day soon, my darling, I shall give you better than beauty.'

Seven times each day she kicked Boy Gwion. 'Don't you

ever go stealing that broth, brat. The day you do is the day you die.'

Boy nodded. He was always hungry, but not so hungry that he wanted to taste the horrible slop in the bronze cauldron.

At all hours of day and night the witch's hooves scuffed the floor as she brought things from the forest and things from the pond, things from the hedgerow and things from the drain; dry things and wet things, cold things and hot. She fed that cauldron till its brew bubbled treacly, close to the brim. 'Stir it and don't stop,' she told Boy, 'But not a taste, not a lick, for the day you do is the day you die.'

Boy shrugged. He had no wish in the world to taste the brew in the cauldron.

One night the Old White Sow was merrier than usual. 'Nearly there, nearly there,' she crooned to Afagddu, as she tucked him into bed. 'Soon now, I know it!' She put on her cloak and took down her basket from the roofbeam. 'Stir, brat! Stir!' she told Boy, and with one more kick, scuffled out into the dark.

Boy stirred with one hand and held his nose with the other, while next door Afagddu snored. The seething bubbles brought nasty, shapeless things to the surface which sank again with a sigh. There were glittering shapes, too, and threads of scarlet. The cauldron spoon was as long as a broom, but Boy went on stirring and stirring all night.

Just before dawn, a rising bubble burst, and three drops spurted on to Boy Gwion's hand.

'Ow!'

He rammed his thumb into his mouth to ease the pain. The three drops left three tastes on his tongue: sweet, salt and sour. Then, into Boy's head burst three stars, and he reeled and staggered and fell.

He saw hill-forts and earthworks, stone circles and bonfires.

He saw the King, the butcher, the beggar and the maid.

He saw machines that could fly, buildings sky-high and mines as deep as hell; saw guns and geysers of oil.

He saw how and why and when and where and who, and all in the space of his brainpan, like magnesium burning.

He saw the past and how, long ago, the witch had stolen him from his cradle. He saw the present and how, that very moment, she was coming up the path. He saw the future and how she would kill him for what he had done. All time was inside him, as well as words in millions – as many as the stars – all waiting to be said.

The Old White Sow pushed open the door with a grunt. She saw at once what had happened. 'Wretch! Rascal! Robber! That was for Afagddu! That was for my boy!' She snatched up the ladle and carried a slopping scoop through to her son, splashing it, hot, into his open mouth. But all the liquor's magic had been in those three drops that burned Boy's thumb. The moment of perfection was past, and Afagddu would have no genius to make up for his ugliness.

Before the witch came back from the bedroom, Boy Gwion fled through the open door. He had glimpsed the mysteries of magic now, and he knew how to change his shape. So he ran his hands through his hair, until his hair turned to ears; he stretched out his body and ran . . . into the shape of a hare.

The Old White Sow came after him, turning herself into a greyhound, the better to catch him.

'Stop and stay, thief,' she barked, 'for if you've seen the future, you know that I shall kill you!' Her lean and bony body gained on the hare, jaws agape and tongue lolling. A river lay in their path. Boy was trapped.

Feeling hot breath on his back, Hare Gwion read magic words off the inside of his eyelids and, speaking them aloud, turned himself into a fish. *Plop*, the squealing hare splashed into the water – a glitter of scales, a flutter of fins – and swam away. The greyhound tumbled in behind.

But as she sank, the Old White Sow turned herself into an otter. A lithe writhe of sleek brown fur sped through after the fish, claws ripping the water to foam. The fish flickered through a streaming forest of weed; his dappled back almost invisible over the mottled riverbed. But the otter only came on, with ravenous jaws.

'Stop and stay, villain, for if you've seen the future, you know I shall eat you!'

In his terror, Fish Gwion leapt clear out of the water, and hearing magic words pound in his ears, he spoke them aloud – and turned into a bird. Steep as a lark he soared into the sky. But the Old White Sow only shook the water off her back and turned herself into a hawk. High as the treetops, high as the hilltops, high as an arrow can be shot, flew Bird Gwion. But between him and the sun, casting a cold shadow over him, stooped the hawk-witch, talons spread.

'Stay and die, filcher,' she shrieked, 'for if you have seen the future, you know that I shall swallow you down!'

Down.

Down swooped Bird Gwion, in at the gaping door of a barn, down on to the threshing floor where harvested ears of corn lay waiting to be threshed. Every ear held a hundred grains, and each grain exactly like every other. Feeling his heart thud out magic words, Bird Gwion spoke them aloud and . . . changed himself into a grain of corn: one grain among a million.

But grain cannot run.

Bck-bck-bck.

The witch turned herself into a chicken and came strutting into the barn. She pecked from morning till night. Scratch-peck. Scratch-peck. 'Lie there and die, Grain Gwion, for if you have seen the future, you know I shall . . . *bck-bck-bck.*'

The grain that was Boy Gwion went down the chicken's throat. She stretched up her head and crowed in triumph, then shook off her feathers and went home to where the cauldron stood cold and congealing.

Did you know, did you know, that grains grow in the dark?

Nine months later, the Old White Sow put a hand to her great belly and gave a scream, like a chicken before its neck is wrung.

'*Is there no ridding the world of that thieving Boy?*'

She gave birth to a child so beautiful that his forehead shone like bronze and his small hands plucked music from the witch's lank hair.

His brightness hurt the witch's eyes. She bundled her baby into a sack and slung it over her shoulder. 'Wretch! Thief! Slave! I will not love you! I shall not love you! Let no one say I ever gave you life!' Then she went to the river, where, as an otter, she had chased Fish Gwion, and she flung her baby into the water to die.

Currents caught the sack, eddies spun it, and the undertow dragged it down into dark, drowning depths. It rolled over the stones where the salmon spawn, it washed over the weir where the salmon fishermen fish. And there the sack was found by the King's own fisherman, wound three times round with golden fishline.

They called the baby Taliesin, which means 'bright brow': a child so handsome that the King prized him in the way he prized the work of his goldsmiths. But only when Taliesin opened his mouth did the King realize what riches had come to him in a hessian sack. For Taliesin the poet spoke of the past, present and future, of how, why, when, where, and who. And when he sang songs, to the music of the King's harpist, he had at his beck words in millions, as many as the stars and twice as bright.

The Battle of the Drums

A NATIVE AMERICAN MYTH

THERE were magical marks on his forehead, and magic in the way he grew – from baby to child in the beat of a heart, from child to youth in another. Lone Man had magical powers, so when he wanted a thing he was inclined to take it. He wanted a coat, and Spotted Eagle Hoita had one, a fine white one. Lone Man whistled up the wind and sent it to blow on Hoita, and the white hide coat was whisked from his back and carried away, away and away.

It blew through the arch of a rainbow which touched it with seven colours along with a glisten of dew. When travellers found it, they said, 'This is so beautiful it must belong to Lone Man.'

So Lone Man came by his coat, but in doing so, he made an enemy. For Hoita *knew* the coat was his. And Hoita also knew how to bear a grudge.

Soon afterwards, there came from the north the beat of a drum like the thud of a heart. It woke the animals on the plain, and stirred them to their feet – every buffalo and dog, every quail and coney and mouse. Every day, Lone Man saw them pass by his home – a huge migration of animals, their colours fading to a whiteness, their white forms fading into the northerly distance. Then his stool stirred its three legs and walked away, whitewash white, along with his hogan and hives, his fishing rod and shoes.

Day and night: *thum-thum-thum*. Night and day: *thum-thum-thum*. Powerless to resist, the animals moved north towards the sound, towards the place called Dog Den. When even the growing things on the plain began to grow pale, Lone Man knew he must act before his people starved. So he turned himself into a little white hare, and loped away north in the footprints of the rest.

When he reached Dog Den, the noise of drumming filled the air from snow to sky, from drift to cloud, filled Lone Man's ears and set his long feet thumping. There was Hoita, leading the animals in a dance, chanting out famine, chanting out strife.

> 'Lone Man shall have his coat;
> Lone Man shall have no more;
> Lone Man shall have no food or joy
> From hill to shining shore.'

The drum Hoita beat was a huge roll of hide taken from the largest buffalo in the world.

> 'Lone Man shall have no luck;
> Lone Man shall have no chance;
> Lone Man shall have no powers at all
> While Hoita leads the dance.'

Now Lone Man knew what he must do: find a drum bigger and more magical than Hoita's. He searched the world over, then he searched the world under, and there he found the two Turtles who swim with the Earth on their back, balancing the world on their shells.

'If I were to beat on your shells,' said Lone Man, 'I could raise magic enough to overpower Spotted Eagle Hoita.'

'If you were to beat on our shells, the world might tumble from our backs and sink into the Waters like a stone in a pond,' replied the Turtles. 'But you are quite right. Our shape has magic enough. Look carefully, Lone Man, and copy what you see.'

So Lone Man felled an oak tree and built a frame. He took the hides of a hundred buffaloes, and stretched them over the oak frame. And he made a drum the shape of an Earth Turtle, and almost as big. When he beat it, the sea quaked, the sky vibrated, the hills jumped and hopped like fleas around the plain. It sounded like the heartbeat of the Earth itself.

'What is that sound?' said Hoita, far away at Dog Den in the north. 'Go and see, Coyote.'

So Coyote went to see what was making the noise. But Lone Man was waiting, and put a lead round his neck.

'What *is* that sound?' said Hoita. 'Go and see, Birds.' So the Birds went to see what was making the sound. But Lone Man was waiting with nuts and seed, to feed them.

'WHAT *IS* THAT SOUND?' demanded Hoita. 'Go and see, Buffaloes.' So the Buffaloes went to see what was making the noise, and the magic of the Great Drum scattered them across the Great Plain, scattered them once again within reach of Lone Man's hungry people, where they were needed most.

The Hoita realized that the sound was not the Earth's heartbeat but the beat at the heart of Lone Man's magic, and he let all the animals go, sent them south again, to recover their colours and roam the lands of Lone Man and his kin.

Spotted Eagle Hoita had glimpsed the future, and knew how much the plains people were going to need Lone Man.

> '*Lone Man shall need my coat;*
> *Lone Man shall need his lance.*
> *The dangers ahead are many*
> *For this leader of the dance!*'

Cupid and Psyche

A ROMAN MYTH

How could anyone be more beautiful than the goddess of love? Unthinkable, or so Venus thought. But then thought was not her greatest strength. She was all passion, all instinct, all rash impulse and emotion. There is a cool, deep stillness in a thoughtful woman, which attracts like a deep lake on a hot day. Perhaps that is why mortal Psyche's quiet, pensive beauty was so appealing. Some said she was even more beautiful than Venus, the goddess of love.

'Kill her!' Venus told her son. 'Chain the wretch to a rock and let's see how lovely she is after Typhon has chewed on her!'

Venus's son, Cupid, was accustomed to being sent on errands by his mother. Armed with his bow and quiver of golden arrows, he would lie in ambush, on her behalf, and fire into the heart of man or woman an arrow tipped with the poison of love. But to wound someone with love was one thing: chaining them to a rock to feed a sea monster was different. Cupid went about his task with horror and disgust. Psyche struggled and pleaded with him. 'Who told you to do this? Who hates me this much?' The golden arrows were spilled across the barnacled rock, and Cupid scratched himself in gathering them up. But obedient to his mother, Cupid overpowered the girl and left her there, silently weeping. The sea writhed in blue-green coils around the bare rock.

Typhon smelled the small, sweet, subtle smell of Psyche

and started up from the deep-sea trench. Its back and wings were black-feathered like the cormorant, its bulk so great that the ocean churned up its sandy bed, and undersea volcanoes erupted. Jaws agape, Typhon came for its puny meal. Fishy breath blasted the trees on shore, and Psyche, pale as snow, closed her eyes.

Suddenly she felt a new wind, fresher and sweeter. The chains around her turned to flowers, and the rock beneath her feet was suddenly a distant speck on a blue mirror. Zephyrus the Breeze had lifted Psyche and was flying with her through the sky. He carried her to a palace where the sound of the sea whispered everlastingly through whorled walls of shining shell.

Zephyrus himself had no shape. So whose were the steps that echoed each night through the seashell palace? Psyche feared them at first, feared she had been abducted by some monster or collector of pretty women. But when, after several days, she had seen no one, she became easier in her mind, and settled to thinking, which made her happy. So did the flowers which she found every day outside her door.

Then one night, the echoing footsteps came to the side of her bed and out of the darkness a voice said, 'It was I who rescued you from the rock, Psyche. I love you, and I want you for my wife. But you must never see me, never see my face.'

'Are you Zephyrus?' she asked.

'He only brought you here to my palace. Don't ask my name. Don't try to see my face, or we shall be lost to each other.'

Psyche thought for a moment. 'I never cared about anything but the beauty of a person's mind and soul,' she said. 'If in a while I find you are as kind and gentle as you seem, I shall be your wife and never wish for the sun to shine on us both.'

Psyche and her mysterious lover knew nothing but happiness within the seashell palace. For a time, Psyche barely thought about anyone else, anywhere else. But she knew that her parents must think her dead, eaten by the sea monster. So one day she asked to be allowed to visit them, to set their minds at rest. Her lover did not want her to go, feared her going, but he did not try to keep her a prisoner. 'You may go,' he said. 'Only promise me you will pay no attention to your sisters if they try to turn you against me.'

Zephyrus kindly carried Psyche home to her father's house, where the family were overjoyed to see her alive – oh, so much more than alive! By the time she had finished describing her life at the seashell palace, her sisters were sea-green with envy. 'Free to do as you like all day? Showered with presents? He must be really hideous, that lover of yours, or he could have had *anyone!* You should take a look – just one peep – see what an ogre you've won for yourself. Why don't you?' But when they looked up, Psyche had gone, gone with the wind.

Still, Psyche was a thinker, a ponderer and puzzler over riddles. Her fingers told her that her mysterious lover was not furred or scaley, warty, feathered or clawed. His face was smooth between her hands. He felt like a perfect young man. So why must she never see him? Every day her curiosity grew until, at last, she could bear the mystery no longer. So when he was asleep, deep asleep, his breathing slow and steady, she crept to the lamp and lit it, carried the lamp to the bedside and let its gentle light fall on his face. '*You!*'

Oozing from the lamp like great tears, three fat drops of oil fell on to the chest of the sleeping man. His lids lifted; the pupils of his eyes contracted; his mouth opened to reproach her. 'What have you done?' Then he was gone.

Gone, too, were the seashell palace, the bed, the flowers, the lamp. They melted away. Psyche found herself on the dark surface of the cold world, all alone. Her foolishness had returned her to the very rock where she had awaited death.

Once again Typhon scented the small, sweet smell of Psyche, but she was too impatient to wait for death in Typhon's jaws. In her despair, she threw herself into the seething sea.

'Oh no!' said the wave. 'I will not drown you!'

'Live, Psyche!' said the saltwater. 'I will not kill you.'

'Go, Psyche!' said the sea. 'Your death would stain me black with shame. You must find some other way to die!' And an arching wave flung her ashore.

Refused permission to die, Psyche resolved to live. She turned her wet face towards the rainy sky. 'I shall never rest till I've found you!' she shouted, she who had never raised her quiet voice. After that nothing frightened her.

She searched hill and plain, mountain and valley. She took ship and sailed the seas, even beat on the doors of the Underworld to ask if her lover were there. From Pole to Pole and through the core of the Earth she searched.

And the gods watched from their mountaintop.

Psyche visited every temple, laying sacrifices on the altar, praying aloud for help to find her lover. At last she came to the temple of the goddess of love, and never suspecting Venus's hatred for her, went inside.

'No! Not there!' cried the gods out of Heaven, but Psyche did not hear.

'Oh dear goddess, loveliest of the Immortals, protector of all those who truly love. Help me find him! Help me, please!'

Behind her, Venus became gradually visible, like a spider's web in the morning dew. 'There, there. I will, child, I will! Dry your tears! Of course I shall help you find your lover . . . just one thing. *You must be my slave for seven years.*'

Such torments and trials, such cruelties and dangers Venus poured on Psyche's lovely head that the gods on Olympus covered their eyes. For seven years Venus sent her slave on errands to the hearts of volcanoes, to the bottom of the sea. She sent her to winnow sand and to dig quicklime, to gather bird's eggs from cliffs and to sweep marshes dry. Psyche did it all.

And every day the gods liked Venus a little less and admired Psyche a little more.

'You see how she does everything that's asked of her!' said Cupid to Jupiter, King of gods.

'Someone's helping her, that's how,' protested Venus sulkily. 'She could never do it alone.'

'You see how she brings a smile to the very faces of the Dead,' said Cupid to Jupiter.

'Silence, son!' raged Venus. 'It's you I sent to kill her in the first place! Why aren't you down there now, setting dogs on her trail, loosing monsters on to her scent?'

'*Because I love her, Mother,*' said Cupid. All Heaven gasped in astonishment. '*Because it was I who rescued her. And it is I who have helped her survive your spite!*' He showed the three small burns on his chest, where Psyche's oil lamp had spilled. 'That's why I beg you, my Lord Jupiter: *make my love immortal!*'

All eyes turned to Jupiter, King of the gods.

'*NO!*' said Venus.

'*YES!*' boomed the god. 'Thanks to Venus's cruelty, Psyche has earned her place among the Immortals. Marry her, Cupid, and when her mortal part falls away I shall set her in the night sky – a bouquet of stars in the arms of the night!'

That is how Psyche's long search ended. Cupid simply walked down from the foothills of Olympus and took her in his arms.

But what Cupid had forgotten – and Venus, too – was the monster Typhon. Woken and rising still from the seabed, with oily feathered wings of black it broke surface now, its thousand jaws snapping; it found no tasty morsel of mortal chained to the sea rock. So it dragged itself ashore, lumbered out of the sea, and came looking for its old enemies – the gods. Its search was a long one, longer than Psyche's. But at last it found a fitting prey: Venus, goddess of love, and her son Cupid.

They fled him far and fast, but when nothing else could save them, they changed themselves into little fishes and leapt up into the sky. Starry fishes, they swim still through the reefs of nebullae, the dark pools of space. And no fish in the ocean is as happy as Cupid, because Psyche is there too, as gentle and silent as a sea anemone caressing the liquid night.

Doctor Faust

A GERMAN LEGEND

FAUST, said his friends, was too clever for his own good. Faust, said his enemies, had no respect for God or religion. The truth was, Faust had a thirst for knowledge and would let nothing, friend nor enemy, stand in the way of his learning. So he took for granted nothing his parents told him, nor his teachers, nor even the priests. Instead, he read every book, consulted ancient charts and arts, and dabbled in chemistry.

Soon he could read the language of the stars and twelve other languages besides. Soon he could utter spells, work magic and, when he summoned up the Devil from Hell itself, the Devil came.

He came in the shape of a black dog with blazing red eyes and gaping jaws.

'Too ugly! Leave me!' Faust cried in commanding tones. 'Come back in some other form, or I shall die of looking at you!' And the dog obediently turned and went. In that instant, Faust felt as powerful as God himself, for he could command the Devil and the Devil obeyed.

When the Devil reappeared, he called himself Mephistopheles and had a human shape, though his face was the saddest Faust had ever seen and there was a look in his eyes like a lost child. 'Why do you summon me, Faust? What do you want?'

'Knowledge,' said Faust. 'Knowledge and power! Everything you can give me that plain, ignorant men cannot have!'

'I can give you that,' said Mephistopheles. 'But everything has a price. You won't want to pay mine.'

'Name it!' said Faust, drunk with his own daring.

'Very well. For twenty-four years I serve you – do anything you ask, fulfil your every wish. After that time, I shall have your soul. Is that agreed?'

All his life Faust had been cleverer than anyone he met, able to outwit the sharpest wit. Here was a dog in human shape. Surely he could outwit him too – take the magic but keep his soul – especially after twenty-four years of learning to be cleverer still. 'Agreed,' he said.

From beneath his cloak, the Devil produced a scroll of paper. 'Sign to it.'

'Of course.'

'*In blood.*'

While the blood was still wet, Faust was already asking questions. How many stars? How large the universe? How old the sun? How does a bee fly? Who rules the universe?

'That last I shan't answer,' said the Devil sulkily.

'Then God is greater than you?'

'Do you like pretty women?' asked Mephistopheles, changing the subject.

He fetched for Faust the most beautiful woman in the history of the world. (At least he fetched a likeness of her, which Faust could admire but not touch, an illusion rather than flesh and blood.) He played tricks on Faust's enemies. He did conjuring tricks for Faust's friends. Anything Faust could think to ask for, Mephistopheles did for him. Having seen the most beautiful woman in the world, of course, no other real, live woman could interest Faust. So he took no wife, no one who would care what became of him. But what did that matter? He had everything else.

He had more money than he could spend; houses and clothes, coaches and castles. But as for knowledge, all he found out was that facts bored him and the truth scared him: that good men went to Heaven, whereas bad men went to . . .

'Help me, books! How am I to trick my way out of this deal?' But his books told him nothing. 'Help me, Wagner! How can I save my skin?' But his serving man did not know, and seeing Faust afraid of some impending doom, Wagner fled his master.

The days went by like bees on the wing, each stinging Faust into an awareness of his terrible predicament. Suddenly he was a middle-aged man, fat and slow from eating the Devil's rich food, lonely and bowed down under all the facts he knew. Faust's contract with Mephistopheles was due to expire, and suddenly Mephistopheles was not so harmless or helpful. Beyond his lonely, red-rimmed eyes, Faust could glimpse a bottomless fiery pit bigger than the universe itself, a black-cogged machine whirring like the workings of an everlasting clock. At midnight, Faust must forfeit his soul to the Devil.

That last night, he considered the money, the laughter, the luxuries, the learning . . . and all of it seemed worthless alongside his little soul. He thought of hiding, of arguing, of pleading, but he knew that the Devil was coming to collect what was owed, and would not leave without it.

He barricaded the door, he loaded a gun, he stopped the clock. But time still moved on unstoppable. Ten o'clock, eleven, twelve. As the clock began to strike, Faust fell on his knees, sobbing and mouthing prayers. But the words turned to pitch in his mouth, and the contract in his pocket burned like phosphorus.

'Turn me into water drops and sprinkle me over the ocean,' he prayed, 'but don't let me fall into the Devil's hands! Don't let him take me to Hell!'

The clock in answer struck the twelfth stroke of midnight. Beneath the floorboards there was a roaring fire. Beyond the curls of smoke issuing between the floorboards, Mephistopheles stood – locked door or no locked door –

holding the contract unfurled. The blood of Faust's signature was still wet . . .

'No. No! *No! No! NO!*'

Next morning Faust was nowhere to be found. Neighbours told of shrieks and cries, of lightning flashes and blood-red rain. But of Faust there was no trace, no bone, no hair. No books written, no sons or daughters to outlive him, no loyal friend to remember him. Nothing remained of the man who had been Faust; only wild stories of screaming in the night, and a slight smell of brimstone near the broken clock.

Alone

A NATIVE AMERICAN MYTH

A WOMAN lived on the shores of the sea. Her name was Copper Woman, though she was made of flesh and bones: flesh and bones and loneliness. One day she was so lonely that she wept, and then, to her shame, was seen weeping by a band of travelling women.

'Don't be ashamed, Copper Woman. Loneliness is not a crime; nor is crying,' said the women. 'There is even magic in a woman's tears. Didn't your crying fetch us here to cheer you?'

It was true. While the visitors stayed, Copper Woman was blissfully happy – talking, laughing, asking questions about the rest of the world, answering questions about her daily life.

'I catch bass here, gather seaweed there, and this is where the best shellfish grow. I made this dress from the silver skin of a seal, this soup from seaweed . . .'

But when the travelling women left, Copper Woman felt more lonely than ever, because now she knew how it felt not to be alone. She stood on the shore and wept, and her tears wetted the sand more than the sea ever had.

Remembering the magic the women had taught her, Copper Woman scooped the wet sand into a little shell and left it on the tide-line. By next day it had grown, not into any recognizable shape, but too large for the shell. So she transferred it to a sea-urchin's shell, then to a crab's. One day it reached out a tiny hand and clasped her finger tight, and would not let go, so that she had to carry it with her everywhere. She brought it shellfish to eat and fish stock, gull-bones to play with as well as bright pebbles and seal's fur.

Copper Woman had given life to Sand Man, and when he was fully grown, his muscles were ropes of sand, strong to help with the fishing, tender to embrace her. Laughing with delight, she worked alongside her mate, chattering and singing, telling him all about herself and the shoreline, asking questions but never waiting for an answer, so glad was she of his company. They slept together in a big bed of sealskins, pillowed on gull feathers. His face was whiskery against hers, like a sea-lion's, and his chest had a soft, silvery fur. Copper Woman thought she would be happy for ever, now that she had a friend.

'I love you,' she said, kissing her handsome Sand Man.

He smiled and turned towards her, his eyes bright with affection. He opened his mouth and she listened eagerly for him to say he loved her too.

But the only sound which emerged was the shrill cry of a seagull. '*Awwwkkhh! Awwwkkhh!*' Sand Man was, after all, the stuff of shells and birdbones and weed; of sand and tears and wishing. Copper Woman cried as she had never cried before, and was lonelier than she had been when she worked alongside the sobbing sea.

The Golden Vanity

AN ENGLISH LEGEND

THE PENNONS at the masthead were new, the gold paint on the figurehead gleaming, and the sailors were still thinking of home when it happened. Not three weeks out of Portsmouth the *Golden Vanity* was overtaken by a Turkish caravel, light and fast and with guns enough to send the ship and all its crew to the bottom of the sea.

Slow and ponderous, the great English treasure galleon wallowed on the swell, while stone balls and chain-shot smashed away the spars and rigging like twigs falling from a tree. 'We're lost! We're taken!' groaned the Captain, and he cursed his crew, his vessel and the admiral who had sent him on this fatal voyage.

Up jumped the cabin boy, Billy. 'There's something I could do, sir! There's something I could try! What would you say to me sinking the Turk deep down where the whale bones lie?'

'I'd say five thousand pounds and marry my daughter,' said the Captain surlily, 'but since when did cabin boys win battles?'

From his belt Billy pulled a little bradawl, a tool for boring holes in wood. 'What say I swam across and holed the Turks under the waterline – let in the sea to wet their heathen feet?'

The Captain threw aside his spyglass and turned to look at the boy for the first time. 'Reckon you could do it?'

'He can if anyone can!' exclaimed the second mate. 'The lad swims like a fish, he does!'

Cannonfire like the crack of lightning rived the smoky air, and a ball whistled by the Captain's ear. He put out a paw and clasped Billy's little hand in his. 'Then do your best for us, son, and do your worst to them!'

They tied a rope round Billy's waist and lowered him into the sea: he trembled like a fish on a line. But no sooner was he in the water than he untied the rope and struck out strongly, gliding through the wavetops like a very porpoise. 'Tell your daughter I shall buy her a fine house with five thousand pounds!' he called back with a laugh.

The water was cold. Now and then it exploded into spray as a cannon-ball fell short or a piece of rigging crashed down into the sea. But by closing his eyes and imagining – Billy the Beau! Little Billy Gentleman! – he somehow reached the Turkish hull. She had heaved-to to empty her cannon into the *Golden Vanity*, and the hull stood still in the choppy ocean. Holding his breath, he dived – clawed away the pitch and tallow coating, and bored through the wooden hull.

Again and again Billy dived, until his lungs were burning and his body blue with cold. Not until he heard the cries aboard the caravel – 'Awash! Awash! We're holed!' – did he push the bradawl back into his belt and begin the long swim back.

Chilled to the marrow and tired past all enduring, Billy closed his eyes and thought of his mother's face the day he rode to church in a carriage, to marry the Captain's daughter; frock coat of red velvet, with a spyglass and a shiny sword, his brothers would say, 'There goes our little Billy; he saved the day, you know!' When he opened his eyes again, the hull of the *Golden Vanity* loomed huge above him, steep as a cathedral wall.

'Throw down a rope, Captain!' he called, and saltwater

slopped into his throat. 'I can't . . . much longer . . . so tired.'

'Raise the topsail and let's put on some speed, men!' said the Captain on his bridge.

The crew stared at him. They ran to the rail. They pointed to Billy, in case the Captain had not heard him. Someone ran for a longer rope.

'Billy did no more than his duty, and now you can do yours,' barked the Captain. 'Man the yard-arms, or I'll blow your heads off for scurvy mutineers!' And he actually primed his hand pistols, then and there. As he did so, he muttered. 'Does he think I have money and daughters to spare on the likes of him?'

'For the love of God, Captain! Keep your money and keep your daughter! But pull me up or I'm dead and done for!' called Billy.

The Captain pursed his thin lips, put his spyglass to his eye and watched the crow's-nest of the Turkish ship sink with a fountaining flurry beneath the cold sea waves. 'Lay on more canvas, men,' he said.

Young Billy pulled the bradawl from his belt. His clammy hand slapped the slow-moving hull. 'I should do to you . . .' His face sank once beneath the surface, his sodden clothes seemed to weigh like lead. 'I should do to you as I did to the Turk . . .' He sank a second time and his fist rapped on the moving hull. '. . . but that I love my friends, your crew!' And so saying, he rolled over in the sea, face-down. The bradawl fell away, away out of his hand, down to where the whale bones lie.

The Founding of London

A VIKING LEGEND

THE FOUR sons of Ragnar were playing chess when the news came that their father was dead.

'Dead? The mighty Ragnar Lodbrok?' said Ivar.

'Dead? Greatest of the Vikings?' said Bjorn.

'Who killed him?' said Hvitserk.

'How, when he wore his magic shirt?' said Sigurd.

They listened in horror to how Ella, King of Northumberland, had routed the army of Ragnar, captured the noble old warrior and thrown him into a pit of snakes. 'At first the snakes could not pierce the shirt, it's true,' panted the messenger. 'But at last Ella guessed there was magic in it and had it torn from your father's back . . . Then the snakes, oh the snakes . . . !' The messenger broke down and wept at the memory of it.

But Ivar had no time for tears. 'Lift me on to my shield, brothers, and may the gods shut me for ever out of the halls of Valhalla if I do not destroy this Ella of Northumberland!'

'Too late! Too late!' wailed the messenger. 'His army is close on my heels – his and a dozen armies besides! They outnumber us twenty to one! The glory of the Viking eagle is falling, falling!'

'My oath is sworn!' replied Ivar. 'I must fight.'

Ivar, crippled from birth, was lifted on to his shield. Each brother held it high on one hand while with the other he drew his brazen sword. Raised up high, Ivar wielding his archer's bow was a rallying point for the Viking warriors.

He loosed arrows like rain in a storm, and every one found its mark.

But Ella's army was huge. Among his allies was King Alfred of high renown, and soon the Norsemen for all their bravery were utterly defeated. Bjorn and Hvitserk and Sigurd set their brother down at the feet of King Ella like a payment of ransom, and the haughty King spat on him.

'Do you admit defeat?'

'We do,' said Ivar.

'Am I the victor?'

'You are,' said Ivar. 'And I swear I will never raise weapon against you, if you will grant me just one boon in your mercy.'

'What is it?' snapped Ella suspiciously.

'As much of this sweet land of England as may be enclosed by the skin of an ox, a little ox.'

Ella beamed magnanimously. 'One ox skin? Take it. That should give you just enough ground to be buried in, ha ha!'

An ox hide was brought, and a sharp knife, too. Ivar began to cut the hide into the thinnest of strips.

'What are you doing?' said Ella uneasily.

'No more than you permitted,' Ivar replied.

Thousands of strips he cut from that one ox hide. On the banks of the River Thames, Bjorn laid down the first. Hvitserk laid another end-on to it. Sigurd placed a third. End-to-end the strips were laid, along and along the green watermeadows . . . over several hills, across a bridge, round the houses clustered by the river. By the time the last strip of skin met with the first, the sons of Ragnar had encircled thirty acres of prime land, and laid claim to the Middle Thames.

King Ella was furious, but what could he do? He had given his word. As he watched the four brothers and their defeated army build a wooden city-stronghold in the middle of his kingdom, he comforted himself that Ivar had given his word too: never to fight him again.

They called the city Lunduna Berg, which became London, in time. There Ivar Lodbrok made his home, at the heart of Ella's empire, though his brothers went back to Denmark. He did not sit idle. He did not chafe at his confinement within these wooden walls. During his childhood, while other boys played, sickly Ivar had studied the magic of the runes. Now he cast the runes all day long, and the Saxons outside his walls heard the click of these mystical stones which could foretell the future: *click, click, click*.

Every day, Ivar propped himself against the city wall and talked to the Saxons who went past. 'Drink my health tonight, won't you, at the inn?' he would say and throw down a gold coin. 'Please accept this small wedding gift,' he would call as a wedding party danced by, and throw down his jewelled cloak clasp. 'Would you care to dine with me?' he would say to the starving beggars curled up against the palisade. The music of his minstrels carried far beyond the bounds of Lunduna Berg.

Ella meanwhile ruled with cruelty and spite. He taxed the people till they groaned, he worked them till they dropped. He quarrelled with his allies, brawled with his ministers and sacked the generals in his army.

'How goes the world with you?' Ivar called down genially from his city's wooden towers.

'Worse than bad,' came the reply from hungry Saxons driving skinny cattle out to plough ground as stony as Ella's heart.

'That's the trouble with kings,' Ivar would murmur. 'Kings take the credit for victories but never take the blame for the bad times.' Little by little, he and his fellow Londoners befriended the Saxons . . . and having befriended them, stirred them up to rebellion!

'*You* should lead us! *You* should be our king,' the Saxons were soon saying. But Ivar always shook his head.

'I gave my word never to fight Ella. I cannot break it.'

'Listen to him! Such an honourable man!'

Ivar smiled. '*I* gave my word . . . But, of course, my brothers never did . . .' So the unhappy Saxons sent word to Denmark, begging Bjorn and Hvitserk and Sigurd to come back and save them from Ella's tyranny. When the brothers landed, everyone rallied to their eagle flag.

This time there was no King Alfred to fight at Ella's side, no alliance of nations, no army of thousands. Though Ivar kept his word and never raised a bow against him, Ella was utterly defeated. It was the enemy within which beat him – an enemy citadel built at the heart of his own kingdom, yes, but also that cruel snake-pit of a heart within his barbarous breast.

The Monster with Emerald Teeth

A MAYAN MYTH

EVEN THE gods make mistakes. First they populated the world by carving little wooden men and women. But the carvings were so badly behaved that their very belongings rose up against them. Their knives stabbed them, their chickens pecked them, their houses fell on them, their millstones ground them to splinters.

But the giants who replaced the wood-men were no better. Vukub-Cakix and his two sons, Earth-Mover and Earth-Shaker, were proud, vain and cruel. Even after the gods had produced their masterpiece – humankind – the three giants made life a misery for everyone on earth. They had to be got rid of. But how?

The heavenly twins, Hun-Apu and Xbalanque were sent to rid the earth of the three giants, and went at once to the nanze tree where Vukub-Cakix picked fruit each day. Hiding in the branches, they waited till Vukub had climbed right to the top of the tree before levelling their blowpipes and taking aim.

'Owowo!' cried the giant, and fell, clutching his face. Though he crashed to the ground like a meteorite, the fall did not kill him. Indeed, now he could see strangers in his fruit tree, he came after them, silver eyes flashing, grinding his emerald teeth. He grabbed Hun-Apu's arm and pulled it clean off before the heavenly twins were able to make their getaway.

'I need it back!' said Hun-Apu when they stopped running. 'I can't go back to Heaven without my arm!'

'Don't worry,' said Xbalanque. 'But now our friend the giant has the most fearful toothache. Our darts hit him in the mouth.'

'I'm not feeling too good myself,' said his twin.

But they put on cloaks and masks and went to the house of Vukub-Cakix, where the giantess Chimalmat was just roasting Hun-Apu's arm for dinner.

Terrible groans came from the bedroom, for the giant was in agony. 'I'd just reached the top of the tree,' he told his wife, 'when this terrible toothache started up. If it hadn't been for that, I'd've have brought you home both those thieves to eat.'

The twins knocked at the door.

'We were just passing . . . couldn't help hearing . . . wondered if we could help . . .' they told Chimalmat, ' . . . we being dentists.'

She hurried them in to where Vukub lay writhing on his bed, swearing horribly and promising to make the world pay for his misery. Green lights flickered over the ceiling as the firelight reflected off Vukub's emerald teeth.

'Say "aaah",' said Hun-Apu.

'Mmm. Just as I thought. All rotten. Those teeth will have to go,' said Xbalanque, peering into the cavernous mouth.

'But all his power is in his teeth!' whispered Chimalmat in awed tones. 'All his strength! How will he bite off his enemies' heads? How will he grind their bones?'

'We shall give him a new set, of course,' said Xbalanque and began, with pliers, to pull out the emerald teeth one by one. A whole emerald mine never held so many jewels as Vukub-Cakix's mouth.

In place of the emeralds, Hun-Apu and Xbalanque left grains of maize. No more did the green fire flicker on the ceiling, no more did Vukub's silver eyes shine. He faded,

faded, faded, like a fire going out. Powerless to lift a finger, he watched the darkness close in on him like a rising flood and carry his soul away.

'What about my arm!' said Hun-Apu when the twins got outside. Xbalanque threw back his cloak and brandished the limb he had rescued from over Chimalmat's fire. 'A little magic,' he said, 'and you'll be as good as new.' And so he was.

Earth-Shaker was a braggart and a show-off. That made him easy to flatter and easier still to find. When the heavenly twins tracked him down, he was busy juggling three small mountains.

'Stupendous!' exclaimed the brothers, bursting into applause. 'So clever! Such strength!'

Earth-Shaker looked down at them, pleased. 'Yeah. There's no mountain I can't move. Name one, any one. I'll show you. Nothing's beyond me.'

Xbalanque pointed to a distant snowcapped peak. 'That one?'

'Easy,' bragged the giant.

'It must make you hungry, all this pushing and juggling,' suggested Hun-Apu. 'Perhaps we could shoot you something to eat?'

Earth-Shaker liked that idea. He was always hungry, always devouring the wildlife tenderly placed by the gods, in the woodlands and hills. As a flock of macaw flew over, the twins put their blowpipes to their lips and brought down a pair of birds. Then smothering them in mud and baking them over a fire, they presented the meal reverently to Earth-Shaker. They did not mention that the darts in their blowpipes were poisoned with curare, that the mud they had used was poisonous, too. By the time Earth-Shaker had eaten his meal, his head was spinning and his silver eyes were dim. He could barely even see the mountain he was supposed to move.

Xbalanque and Hun-Apu led him there, ignoring his

whimpers, saying that he was trying to worm out of a challenge. 'He can't do it, you see, brother? He was just bragging,' they said.

So Earth-Shaker, in his insane pride, pushed against the mountain till his sweat ran down it in rivers. He pushed so hard that he left hand prints, a fathom deep. But then his heart burst with the strain of so much poison and so much showing off.

Which left only Earth-Mover, proudest giant of them all.

He was nosy by nature. So the heavenly twins dug a pit which looked like the foundations of an enormous house, and waited. When Earth-Mover came along, he at once climbed down to inspect the pit, thinking what a big house must be planned and how he might just take it for himself.

He saw the huge pile of timber logs stacked beside the hole, but he did not realize, until too late, that Xbalanque and Hun-Apu stood behind the logs with crowbars, levering them forward.

One by ten by hundreds, the huge tree trunks tipped, rolled and fell into the pit on top of Earth-Mover. They fell with the noise of an avalanche, and when the noise stopped, all was silent.

'Come one, come all and build on the ruins of the Giants!' declared Xbalanque. 'Build a fine home for yourselves over the broken bones of Earth-Mover; you and your families will be safe now from his bullying!'

The young men did just that. Four hundred of them built a log house big enough for all of them to live in, and when it was built, they had a party to celebrate.

But beneath them, Earth-Mover was not dead at all. He had found himself a crevice safe from the falling logs, and there he had bided his time, silver eyes gleaming, grinding his emerald teeth. At midnight he got to his feet, flinging up his head, flinging out his arms, tossing the house and its four hundred occupants into the night sky. It was like the eruption of a volcano.

So high were the young men thrown, so wide their eyes with terror, that Xbalanque looked up and saw the moonlight glimmer in eight hundred eyes. And in that instant, he transformed the boys into stars to keep them from falling to their deaths.

Heartsick and angry, the heavenly twins worked alone to avenge the young men. They undermined two mountains towering over a deep ravine and, when Earth-Mover walked through the ravine, Xbalanque toppled one mountain on top of him and Hun-Apu toppled the other.

Like a blanket, the rocks and earth rucked and folded over the fallen giant. This time he must surely die! But out between the boulders reached a hand, grasping, clawing. Out through the solid earth burst another. And so Xbalanque and Hun-Apu invoked the magic of the heavens, the magic of the gods which had made the giants a thousand years before.

And Earth-Mover was turned to stone, petrified, stopped stock-still and lifeless in the very act of grasping for life.

The Golem

A JEWISH LEGEND

IN THE course of any day, there are dull, repetitive jobs to be done. The more intelligent the man, the more wearisome routine seems to him. So that when the rabbi, Judah Loew ben Bezabel, contemplated the daily round of cleaning, bell-ringing, winding of clocks, checking of candles, mending of vestments, it seemed to him that no man (or even woman) should waste his God-given life doing it. So he built a creature – without mind, without soul, with little shape and no family – to do all the tedious tasks within the Prague synagogue. He called it the Golem, which means 'lifeless lump of earth'. Under its tongue, Judah put a tablet, and the tablet empowered the limbs to move, the shapeless trunk to heave itself about.

It was hideous to look at, but who would see it? The Golem went about his work in the gloomy unlit synagogue when no rabbi or worshipper was present. It pulled the candle stubs from their sconces and fetched new ones, polished the brass and swept the floor, muttered meaningless words from no living language, as it sewed the vestments, washed the windows and scared cats off the front steps.

Perhaps Judah should have written GOLEM on his creature's forehead. But as it was, he wrote the word he loved best: AMETH, which means truth. Once, when old Mordecai the grocer accidentally caught sight of the creature scrubbing amid the shadows, he gave a cry of, 'Oh! Death has come for me!'

Judah sent the Golem away, and laughed, and soothed the old man's fright. 'It's not Death. That's only my Golem.'

'But he has "Death" written on his forehead!'

'No, no. Not METH, but AMETH,' said Judah, and smiled at the mistake. 'The "A" was hidden in the shadows, you see?'

Through his dull, glintless years, the Golem looked out on a world of stone and brass and wood. Sometimes he heard singing and liked that. Sometimes the sun shone through the coloured window-glass and splashed over the Golem like a shower of gems. His last sight each night was of Rabbi Judah's face, large near his own, fingers reaching into the Golem's mouth to remove the tablet. Then darkness closed over him like a coffin lid.

But one day, Judah Loew ben Bezabel forgot to remove the tablet. (He was an intelligent man, and such routine little jobs tended to slip his mind.) The Golem moved on around the empty hall of the synagogue, though all his tasks for the day had been done. He went to check the steps, but there were no cats. The night street stretched away like a dark corridor, so naturally, he began to sweep it.

The broom wore down to a stump. Dawn came up, and the sun shone full in the Golem's face for the first time.

He went mad with joy.

It was the ferocious joy of the Earth as it shakes down trees and houses. It was the destructive joy of a young child who knows no better than to break things. When people saw the Golem on the streets, they screamed, 'A monster! A ghoul!' and he did not like that. He hurled the people through windows, for the joy of seeing the glass shatter. He hurled carts into the river, for the sake of the splash. The tablet under his tongue suffused his body with more strength than ever before, his rudimentary mind with new thoughts. He must taste more of this new, brighter world!

But the light hurt his eyes, the screams hurt his ears, and he could not find his master. People were throwing things at him now, and firing loud guns. The Golem began dimly to feel pain and fright and rage. He tore the walls out of buildings, looking for Judah. He climbed church spires and threw down clocks and gargoyles. Though they tried to kill him, no one could, because he was never truly alive – a lump of clay.

But then God made Man out of a lump of clay, and Judah had made something very like.

When the statues would not speak to him, the Golem pushed them down. The colourful market stalls intrigued him: he snatched down the awnings. The army got in his way, and so he shooed the soldiers away, like the cats from the synagogue steps.

But where was Judah? The cacophony of a city in panic maddened and amazed the Golem, and he ripped off doors and punched down fences, looking for his master, calling for him in a shapeless language nobody understood.

He was hurt. He was lost. By the time Judah Loew ben Bezabel came running, robes flapping, face aghast, the Golem blamed *him* for the dazzled turmoil of his mind. He left tearing up horse-troughs, and turned on Judah with a grotesque snarl. His shapeless hands closed round the rabbi's throat, and they both fell to the ground.

Judah, half-throttled, saw the world shrink to a dim, half-lit confusion. His strength was puny in comparison with the Golem; he knew he could never fight it off. But with his last conscious thought, Judah reached up and struck the Golem's forehead – smudged out the letter 'A' from the world *ameth*: left the word *meth*: *death*.

The Golem's eyelids flew open; the eyes beneath were not dim, but flashing bright. '*Life, not Death!*' he said, quite plainly, then fell forward with the weight of a horse on top of Rabbi Judah.

I ought to mention: the Golem was only tiny, only waist-high to a real man. You may see for yourself. What remains of the Golem stands in a glass case in Prague Museum, a clay figurine as ugly as sin, the Hebrew for 'Death' still scrawled on his forehead.

Mummy's Baby

AN INUIT MYTH

EVERYONE knows that babies are a treasure. But most have forgotten that once babies had to be come by in the same way: by digging. All sons and daughters lay underground, like spring bulbs: girls near the surface, boys deeper down. And a woman who wanted a family had only to take a spade and go mining. Consequently, strong, fit, hard-working women had whole armies of children, whereas lazy women might have only one or two.

Then there were the accursed women – luckless wives who, dig as they might, never found the treasure they were seeing. Kakuarshuk was just such a woman. More than sleep, more than food, more than sealskin coats or a fine house, Kakuarshuk wanted a baby. But wherever she sank her spade, however deep she dug and for however long, she turned up nothing but ice and snow, lichen and frozen earth. Sometimes it seemed as if she had dug up all Greenland in her search.

In desperation, she went to visit an *angekkok*, a conjuror, who plucked magic out of the air rather than children out of the earth. 'Please tell me!' cried Kakuarshuk. 'Where must I dig to find a child? I've worn out five spades digging, and all I have to show for it is a basketful of loneliness!'

The *angekkok* scratched in the dirt with a magic stick – a map with glaciers and mountains and villages. 'Dig here,' he said, closing his eyes and driving the stick hard into the ground. 'Here or nowhere.'

The place was a great journey from Kakuarshuk's village, but she took nothing with her – only a spade over her shoulder and a great yearning in her heart. Like a goldminer she struck her claim. Like a prospector after diamonds she broke open the hard crust of the earth. No girl baby lay near the surface. But perhaps a boy lay deeper down, waiting for her, with joy clenched in his tiny fists. So Kakuarshuk dug and went on digging. Deeper than any reasonable woman would have dug, deeper than any woman had *ever* dug, Kakuarshuk shovelled up the soil, until the sky was no more than a grey speck high above her head. Through permafrost and fossil layers, rocky strata and soft loam she dug, until like a black mole, she was lost inside the very earth. When her spade broke, she dug on with the shaft until, exhausted, she lay down and waited to die.

A moment later, a spade sliced past her head, and sunlight streamed into her face. Somebody was tunnelling in the opposite direction!

'Oh, yes! Yes! I have found one!' cried a voice. 'A dear little lady one! Oh! Oh! My very own little mummy!'

A baby, huge as a polar bear, as pink and bare as a crayfish and without a tooth in her head, scooped up Kakuarshuk and hugged her close. Overhead, a brilliant blue sky spilled hot sunshine over a green wonderland of flowers and trees. There was no ice, no snow in this land peopled with giant babies. Crawling, toddling, laughing or crying, there were babies everywhere. Some were digging with little trowels, and some had already found what they were after. Here, on the other side of the world, the babies dug for mummies and, having found them, cradled them in their arms, while the mummies grew younger (and wiser) day by day.

It took some getting used to for Kakuarshuk. She was accustomed to working hard all day, and yet here all she had to do was ride in the crook of her baby's arm and be sung to. The babies did everything for their mummies, fetching them food, washing and dressing them, settling them to sleep under the shade of the flickering trees.

She explained, as she was dandled on her baby's knee, about her long journey through the earth, about the differences between her world and this. She told of her longing for a baby of her own. Her baby looked at her with tear-filled eyes.

'When you are young enough, my darling, I shall show you where to dig for your heart's desire. But you will need all your strength, so close those pretty eyes and go to sleep now. There's my good little mummy.'

Kakuarshuk's child was true to her word. One day she took Kakuarshuk to a place called Troll Mountain and gave her a scarlet trowel. 'Dig here, my pet lamb,' said Baby, 'and never give up, come trouble, come terror, come troll. If you are spared, you may see your world again, though I'm sorry to lose you – sorrier than you will ever know.'

Kakuarshuk began to dig. She dug so deep that soon the brink of the hole was no more than a speck of blue high above her. This time she struck a tunnel, and wandered along it, in utter darkness, hoping to find an exit on her own side of the earth. But the tunnel linked with others – with a maze of tunnels – and every one *dug by a troll!*

They pounced on her out of the darkness, huge grotesque beasts as white as slugs, with snuffling noses and blind, white eyeballs. They slashed at her with their long claws, thrashed at her with dead seals and walruses whose tusks made deep and bloody wounds in Kakuarshuk's side.

She ran, while she was able to run, but as more and more trolls attacked, fell to her knees and crawled, sobbing and calling for help. The trolls kicked and rolled her down endless rocky subterranean passageways, but just when she decided her life was at an end, a soft paw closed around her hand and drew her aside into a daylit shaft.

While the blind trolls blundered by, cursing and groping and kicking, the red fox kept its paw to its lips. Then, when they were gone, it helped her upwards, up the shaft of what seemed like a well.

Kakuarshuk lost consciousness as they neared the light. A terrible, irresistible desire to sleep overwhelmed her, and she was afraid that, as she fell asleep, her hand might slip out of the silky paw of her dear red fox . . .

When she woke, she was asleep on the floor of her own hut. Around her were the smiling, familiar faces of her neighbours, making strange gurgling and cooing noises in the backs of their throats.

'They've all become babies while I was away!' she thought, with a moment's panic. Then she realized that there was something in her arms, looked down and saw a little baby boy blearily waking, too: her neighbours were talking to the baby.

'I hear you found yourself a fine son, Kakuarshuk,' said the *angekkok*, putting his head in at the door. 'I wish you joy of him, and few tears.'

Kakuarshuk thought of the other side of the world, and even in that moment of perfect happiness – *because* of that perfect happiness – she knew exactly what had made her mummy-baby cry at their parting.

Dear Dog

A JAPANESE MYTH

God knows, the old man and his wife had little enough to call their own. There was rarely enough food on their plates, enough fuel for a fire, or enough money to repair the roof when it let in the rain. But they did have a dog and a pretty garden, too, and, in those, Sane and Sode believed themselves rich indeed.

A cherry tree grew in the garden – Sane's pride and joy. When it put on blossom in the spring, no princess in all Japan was more glorious. The milky foam of blossom sat like a blessing over the little garden, and every morning Sane and Sode would stand, hand in hand, gazing in rapture.

'Delightful!' said the old man.

'A wonder!' said the old woman.

'Woof,' said the dog, and wagged his tail.

One day, the dog began to dig near the cherry tree. He scrabbled and burrowed until his paws made a hollow scratching on something buried underground.

The chest was ancient – far older than Sane or Sode or even the house where they lived. It was too heavy for the elderly couple to lift, so they opened it where it stood, and there, laid bare to the spring sunlight, were gold coins, gems and chalices, silver spoons and small vases of exquisite alabaster.

As Sane handed the treasures up to his wife, a long shrill whistle sounded beyond the fence. Their neighbour Bozo poked up his head, grinning mouth agape, eyes bulging like marbles. Nothing showed of his nagging wife but one knobbly finger poking and prodding at Bozo's head and a shrill voice demanding, 'What is it? What they got? What they doing? Don't just stand there whistling! Tell me!'

'Please, please, honoured neighbours,' said Sode, 'you must share in our good fortune. Our house is small and our needs are smaller. Please have some of this gold.'

But Bozo was not satisfied with sharing his neighbours' good fortune: he *envied* it horribly. The thought of that mangy dog unearthing a mint of money made him writhe with envy. 'They don't even know how to spend it!' he complained to his wife. 'Now if it were me, I'd know how to make the most of a stroke of luck like that!'

And while Bozo seethed, his wife nagged like a toothache. 'I told you, *we* need a dog like that. What are you going to do about it. Eh? Eh? You've got to get hold of that dog. You've got to get that dog to dig in our garden!'

So in the end, Bozo went round to his neighbours and asked to borrow their beloved dog. And because Sane and Sode never refused anything it was in their power to give, they lent their dear dog to the next-door neighbours.

Bozo shouldered a spade and hauled the dog roughly down his garden by its lead. Pointing at the ground, he snarled, 'Now find treasure, pooch.'

The dog sat down.

'Find treasure, I said!' raged Bozo, instantly furious. The dog whined and lay down, its paws over its nose. '*Find*, you lazy pile of flea-bitten bones!' shouted Bozo, and shook the spade.

The dog rolled on its back and tucked up its paws, as if asking to be tickled. But then, when Bozo only swore and wagged his spade, the dog finally began to dig. He scrabbled and scraped and burrowed till his paws unearthed the lid of a chest – just as he had done next door. Bozo kicked the dog aside and began to dig with his bare hands, scrabbling frenziedly for the padlock and latch.

But as the weary dog dozed, and Bozo threw handfuls of earth at his wife's feet, the chest flew open and all its treasures were laid bare. Worms and weevils, centipedes and millipedes, ants and snails, bugs and slugs burst out of the chest, swarming up Bozo's trouser legs and into his wife's shoes. In his disgust and disappointment, Bozo brought down his spade – thwack, crack – on the dog's head and killed it where it lay.

'The spade slipped. Sorry. Couldn't be helped,' said Bozo as he handed back an armful of dead dog to the heart-broken owners. They wept bitter tears over their dead friend, and buried him under the cherry tree: the most beautiful spot in the garden.

The year grew older, the tree grew taller. Times grew harder for everyone in Japan. Drought reached its gnarled and twiggy hands through all the fields, blighting the rice crop, leaving fish dead in the dried-up river beds.

But the cherry tree was not stunted by the drought. On the contrary, its branches pushed outwards until they were touching the very roof of Sane's dismal old shack. The boards of the walls opened, the tiles of the roof were pushed out of place and the rain poured in.

'I shall have to cut back those long branches,' he said.

'Oh, please don't!' said Sode. 'It would be like maiming a dear friend to set a saw to our lovely cherry tree!'

But by wintertime the safety of the whole house was at risk. Like a great fist, the cherry tree was pushing off the roof, laying open the rooms below to wind and rain and snow. Regretfully, the old man took his saw and cut off the jutting limb. 'At least we shall have firewood for a week or two,' he said.

'No.' Sode was adamant. 'We shan't burn the wood! I feel sure a little of our dear dog is in that cherry. You can make it into a grinding jar for me. That way at least we shall put it to some use, and I'll think of our dear friend every time I grind my rice.'

'What rice?' asked Sane, with a wry smile. 'If this famine goes on much longer, we shall be laying our own old bones down in the dust beside our dear dog. There's no rice to be had for a hundred miles. Not even for gold.'

It was true. By the time he had carved the cherry wood into a grinding jar, Sode had only a handful of rice left in the house. Their gaunt faces looked tenderly at one another over the grinding jar. 'I'm glad our dear dog did not live to suffer and starve with us,' said Sode, and Sade nodded gravely.

Scrrr scrrr scrrr, the pestle ground the rice in the grinding jar. The jar filled with powdered rice – filled and spilled over, making snow-white mounds on the kitchen table. The soul of the dog had indeed fused with the soul of the cherry tree, and his love for his owners was in the very fabric of the jar, making it as magic as the dog himself had been. Not once, but every time Sode used it, the cherry-wood jar filled with food enough for five, so that Sode and Sane were able to feed the whole street.

'I want it. They owe it to us! Worms and slugs, that's all we got from that wretched mutt of theirs. They could at least lend it to us!' carped the woman next door.

'But they are sharing their food with us, my dear,' said her harassed husband, sucking his chopsticks at the end of a good meal.

'Typical! They just give it away!' she raged. 'If you and I

had the only source of food in the whole province, just think! We'd be as powerful as the Emperor himself!' And she did not stop nagging until her husband at last agreed to go next door and steal the magic grinding jar.

A handful of rice was all it took to start the magic, so in went a handful of rice.

And suddenly the room was full of humming, the air black. Flying insects banged clumsily into their faces, crawled into their ears and clothing. Bees and wasps and hornets.

Husband and wife fled – out of the house, across the garden, into the lily pond and out again, through the river and into the woods. But in their desperate rage, they had achieved one last piece of wickedness. When old Sane and Sode poked their heads in at the open door, worried by the noise, wanting to know if they could help, they saw the blackened shape of their magic grinding jar falling to ashes in the fire grate.

Weeping, Sane swept together all the ash into a pan, and went sadly to sprinkle it on the grave of his dead dog. 'If your spirit was in the vessel,' he said aloud, 'it returns to you now, little friend. Be happy.'

The weather was cold. The drought had lasted all summer and autumn; now even the dark snowclouds refused to slake the earth's thirst. And yet surely that was snow on the boughs of the cherry tree? Surely there were snowflakes whirling in the bitter wind? Either snow or . . . *blossom?*

How could there be blossom in winter? How could the flowers bloom and the fruit be taking shape in the orchards? How could the rice plants be spiking green through the bleak bare landscape, turning the whole countryside a cheerful green? The cherry tree in the old couple's garden foamed with so much blossom that the whole town came out to see it. On their way out to the fields to reap a miraculous harvest, on their way to celebrate with friends and neighbours, they stopped and stared open-mouthed at the cherry tree, a fountain of petals splashing the sky with pink and white.

Monkey Do:
The Story of Hanuman

A HINDU MYTH

FOURTEEN thousand giants Prince Rama slew in a
single day, and the only one left alive crawled to the
feet of Ravana the Demon King, with news of the
defeat.

'All my warriors dead?' raged Ravana, tossing his ten
heads till they cracked together and thrashing the air with
his twenty arms. 'Well, if my fighting men can't kill Rama,
at least I can break his heart! I shall rob him of that perfect
wife of his!' So, mounted in his magic chariot, scorching
the forest with the sparks from its wheels, Ravana
snatched Sita – lovely Princess Sita – by her hair and
carried her off. The sap in the flowers froze at the sight of
it: the birds in the trees choked on their song. Rivers
stopped flowing, and the moon flushed sickly green. 'Sita!
Sita! What is life without Sita?' cried the whole realm of
nature.

Sooner than see Sita in the clutches of the vile Demon
King, the King of Vultures hurled his very life under the
chariot's wheels. The horses shied and smashed loose, the
bladed wheels clashed together like cymbals, and the
chariot sagged, buckled and broke apart.

. . . But Ravana simply took to the air, Sita's hair still
twined around one of his twenty arms, his ten ghastly
mouths laughing aloud. The tree-tops lashed in lament,
parakeets shrieking, monkeys jabbering in the topmost

branches. Seeing a family of monkeys gazing at her with round, stricken eyes, Sita pulled the golden bangles off her wrist and threw them, calling, 'Tell Rama! Tell Prince Rama!'

The monkeys caught the bangles in clever paws and were gone, swinging away under the leaf canopy. Beneath the winged chariot, forest gave way to shimmering sea.

Rama was picking lotus flowers when the Monkey General found him: Hanuman, Chief of Staff to the King of Monkeys and most marvellous of all his breed. 'Stir yourself, my prince! Ravana the Revolting has ravished away your wife! You and I have work to do! My troops and tricks are yours to command, but we must hurry!'

'Where has he taken her?' asked Rama, jumping to his feet.

'No one knows, but my monkey millions are already searching!'

As the monkeys soon discovered, Ravana had taken Sita to the island of Sri Lanka. There, on the highest mountain, he had a palace – a mirage of loveliness built by the gods themselves, but annexed by the ugly and the wicked. Out of the jungles of the world, the monkey millions rallied to Hanuman's battle cry: an army of apes ready to lay down their lives for the lovely Sita. But between them and the Princess stretched the impassable straits of Pamban, swilling with monsters. On the seashore, the frustrated monkey cohorts bared their teeth at the unfriendly sea.

But Hanuman had magic. He wore the very wind in his tail! What is more, he could change shape whenever he chose. There, on the over-crowded beach, he began to grow, until his legs were large as siege engines, flexed like catapults, powerful enough to propel him over surf, over sea, over miles of sea! A veritable mountain of monkey. A great gasp went up from his monkey warriors as Hanuman made that prodigious leap. In a second, he was only a speck in the sky, and a hooting, whooping shout followed him out over the water. But a terrible silence followed.

Out of the ocean depths, bigger than a breaching whale, reared up the head of the Naga-Hag. Green-tressed with slimy seaweed and pocky with barnacles, her mouth gaped, dark, wet and jagged. Powerless to stop himself, Hanuman hurtled inside.

The Naga-Hag meant to chew on Hanuman and swallow him down. But the Monkey General used his magic to grow still larger, wedging his head into the roof of her mouth, his feet into her hollow teeth. And he forced open her jaws as wide as they would go. Then, with a flick of his magic tail, Hanuman was tiny as a flea: he shot out of her ear, leaving her teeth to clash shut on her tongue. '*Ahhooeurghh!*'

Back on the beach, Prince Rama exhorted the monkeys, 'Build me a bridge! A bridge, my friends! We must reach Sri Lanka!'

They built it not from wood or canes, but from clasped hands, linked tails and braced backs. Balancing with acrobatic skill, monkey on monkey on monkey, they bridged the Pamban.

Meanwhile, Hanuman landed – softly, softly, magic monkey – on Sri Lanka, and entered Ravana's palace. His green eyes blinked at the sheer opulence of the Demon King's lair. Everywhere, the walls were studded with gemstones, the doors inlaid with diamonds. Banners of silk rippled at every flagstaff, and Persian carpets draped every wall, while baskets of saffron stained the air gold with blowing pollen, and joss sticks gave off coils of coloured smoke. But no amount of incense could mask the rank, mouldering stench of Evil. And everywhere, in every alcove and dormitory, at every sentry post and turn of the stairs, squatted hideous rakshasas, whose name means 'destroyers'!

'Give me your love, sublime Sita!' Ravana's bullfrog

croak echoed along the cloistered walks. 'Give me your love to feed on!'

Hanuman padded the silk-fringed stairs, poking his nose in at every door, until at last he found the turret where Sita was held prisoner.

As soon as Ravana had gone, Hanuman darted inside. 'Jump on to my back, lady, and I will carry you out of this cesspit!'

'Oh, I can't! I couldn't,' whispered Sita, her lovely cheeks hot with maidenly modesty. 'No man must touch me but Rama my husband!'

'I'm not a man,' Hanuman pointed out. 'I'm a monkey.' But Sita was adamant: even Ravana had held her only by her hair. So there was nothing for Hanuman to do, but wait for the monkey army to cross the Pamban. Nothing to do? Well, while he waited, he could at least kill rakshasas.

Thousands of these vile demons served the Demon King. Some had bulbous bodies and long trailing arms, some elephant trunks or horses' heads. Some were giants with three eyes and five legs; some looked like gorillas but for their blood-red eyes and ginger beards. They infested the palace like rats or cockroaches, and they liked nothing better than a fight. Still, Hanuman took them on single-handedly, and by jumping and weaving, dodging and ducking, narrowly kept out of their claws. Up and down stairs they chased him, along passageways, through cellars and over rooftops. Exhausted, overheated, some dropped in their tracks, wheezing and fanning themselves. 'By the time the Prince arrive,' Hanuman taunted, 'not one of you will have breath enough to whistle!'

But at that moment, a lasso fell round the Monkey General's shoulders, tightened round his throat, and dragged him, sprawling and spitting, under the boot of Ravana's hideous son. 'What shall I do with him, Father? What? Shall I eat him, or tear him limb from limb?'

'Monkey meat is tough,' said Ravana, sneering on all his ten faces. 'Set him alight and let's see him burn!'

Oily rags were tied to the monkey's tail. Sita prayed, her hands over her face, but it seemed nothing now could save Hanuman from a hideous death. Smugly the Demon King held a lighted spill to the monkey's tail; there was a smell of burning fur.

Hanuman seemed to shrivel with the heat. He *was* shrivelling! He shrank down just enough to slip free of the rope binding him, and bounded clean out of the window!

From sill to parapet he sprang, from awning to flagstaff, his blazing tail held stiffly out behind. Silk banners and brocade pavilions were kindled by the burning rag. Squirming in through open shutters and with his tail for a spill, he lit bed-hangings and Persian rugs, tapestries and wicker baskets. Soon the whole palace was ablaze, and 'destroyers' of every shape and smell were jumping from the windows, or sliding down knotted sheets to escape the inferno.

That was when Rama arrived, crossing his bridge of monkeys which dismantled itself behind him into an army. A hundred thousand billion monkeys swarmed over the burning ruins of Ravana's palace, pelting rakshasas with white-hot gemstones.

Ravana was unrepentant. He thumped his chest and bellowed for reinforcements. And out of the sea came the Naga-Hag, out from the mountains came the terrible Kumbha-Karna who could swallow a thousand men at one gulp. Soon Prince Rama was forced to retreat, bleeding from a dozen wounds. Though his courage was undimmed, his strength began to fail. He fell to his knees and his monkey legions re-formed to shield him from a sleet of poisoned arrows.

'Fight on, boys!' cried Hanuman. Once more he transformed himself – into a bird, this time – and flew away. Was he turning tail? Had his burns weakened him? Was he afraid? Not Hanuman! Within the hour he returned, from the flowery slopes of the far-off Himalayas, his paws bunchy with herbs. Tenderly he tended to Rama's wounds, and before Ravana could regroup his shattered army, led his monkey millions into the attack once more.

The gods themselves looked down on that desperate day. Their hearts were stirred by the heroic deeds they saw, and Indra sent down his chariot for Rama to ride in, while Brahma leaned down out of heaven to hand the Prince a single golden arrow.

It was that arrow which finally pierced the heart of Ravana. As it did so, as the fiendish demon crashed to earth, like a gusher of oil, the strangest smell pervaded the battlefield of Sri Lanka. Perfumed flowers of every colour began to rain down out of the clouds, covering the faces of the fallen, lying in drifts upon the ruins of the gutted palace.

Princess Sita stepped into the golden chariot beside her husband, the monkey millions re-formed their living bridge, and Prince Rama drove home over the straits of Pamban, his General dancing on wiry shanks behind him and squealing shrilly for joy.

A Bouquet of Flowers

AN ABORIGINAL MYTH

I T WAS from a piece of the sun that Baiame made the world, but his home was among the stars, and it was there that he returned when his work of creation was done.

'Don't cry, little ones,' he told the people and animals as he said goodbye. 'I have to go. Otherwise you would forever run to me with your troubles – like children never learning to grow up. You know I love you and that I'll still be watching over you from my home.' He pointed to the galaxy of the Milky Way stretched like a silver hammock across the night sky.

The animals nodded their heads and wandered off, far and wide. The men and women also understood, but stayed waving long after Baiame the Creator had risen into the sky. Some lay down on soft clumps of flowers to gaze up at the sky and remember their long talks with the Father Spirit. Then they too got up and walked home, thoughtful, wistful, trailing tardy feet through the flowers which carpeted every fold and furrow of the shining new Earth. Wherever Baiame had trodden, flowers had sprung up: every colour of the rainbow and a thousand shades between – scarlet, umber, purple, gold and white. From horizon to horizon they cloaked the rocky ground, cushioned and pillowed it into the sweetest of resting places.

But what were those flowers feeling now? Flowers have no power of reason, no instinct to guide them. They could not comprehend why dear Baiame, who had given them life, should no longer be nearby.

So some migrated. Like birds in winter, they rose in huge flocks, fledged with their own petals, flying, flying towards the object of their love. Into the sky they fluttered, on outwards into space, swagging the sky with coronas of colour. The rest died.

Soon the air was filled with cries of women searching, searching, then realizing that there was not a single flower left living on the whole bare, brown face of the Earth. The air was filled with something else, too – with swarms of frantic bees searching in noisy millions for one speck of pollen, one sip of nectar. There was no golden honey to be had either, and life was much less sweet in those drab days after the flowers died.

In time, of course, the sadness faded. Those who remembered the flowers grew old. Naturally, they told their grandchildren about them and the wonder that had once been, but the grandchildren hardly believed such far-fetched fairy tales. Those children, as they grew older, remembered talk of flowers, but not, of course their colours. Who can remember something they have never seen, or describe it to their grandchildren? So flowers bloomed only in the mouths of story-tellers – a wonder of times long gone. And colour was only in the skins of animals, in insects and the sky, in fishes and the sea. And in the eyes of the story-tellers.

Watching with gentle multicoloured eyes, Baiame felt sad at this one flaw in the Earth's loveliness. So one night, along with the starlight, he rained down dreams on sleeping humanity. Those with listening hearts were stirred by a voice: they seemed to hear it telling them to make a journey. By first light they set off – like sleepwalkers unable to resist the yearning within them. And every man, woman and child who answered the yearning found that their journey brought them to the selfsame spot. From north and south, near and far, hither and yon they came, to the mountain where Baiame had long ago stepped off into space – and to which he had now returned!

There he sat, reaching out his arms like a father inviting his children to sit on his knee. 'Come with me, little ones,' he said. 'I have something to give you.'

Gathering them up into his hands, into his hair, into the crook of his arm and the folds of his robe, he carried them into the sky and on out into space, to where the Milky Way stretched like a silver hammock. He took them over dunes of darkness to valleys invisible from Earth . . . and their cries of amazement set the stars swinging.

For there lay swathes of colour they had never seen before, colours even their women of vision had not dreamed nor their painters imagined.

'These are the "flowers" your story-tellers speak of,' said Baiame. 'Pick them. Pick as many as you can carry, and take them back with you to the Earth. On the day I took a piece of sun and made the world for you, I meant there to be flowers. You have been without them too long. So take them, and when they die, sprinkle their seed on the brown ground, and I will send warmth and rain enough to make them come again.'

In sheaves and armfuls they reaped flowers and carried them down out of the sky. Like conquering heroes they returned to their separate villages, laden with colour, to astound their families and amaze their friends with bouquets of such dazzling glory that it seemed a rainbow had crashed to Earth and scattered its debris over their homes.

And though Baiame's helpers were not able to carry as many flowers as had once bloomed on Earth, they took enough to paint every corner of the world with every colour in the mind of God.

The Curious Honeybird

A BANTU MYTH

LEZA SAT idly juggling the magic of the world: three calabashes, perfectly round and red, picked from the Tree of Everything.

'Why three?' asked the curious Honeybird.

'How could I juggle with two?' answered Leza. 'Or eight?'

Leza, Lord and Creator of the Bantu people looked down from his plateau of sky. He did not live so very high above the people he had newly created – just high enough to see what they were doing and watch that they came to no harm. He wished them no harm. Indeed, he wished them all the good in the world – which was why he had decided to pick the three calabashes.

'Take these down to First Man and First Woman, Honeybird,' he said, stringing the three scarlet globes around the bird's neck. 'I need both hands free to climb down. Tell them that they may open these two. Tell them I'm coming, and that I will explain how to use what's inside. Also, I'll tell them the purpose of the third . . . Oh, but Honeybird!'

'Yes, master?'

'Mind you don't go opening those calabashes!'

'Would I?' twittered the Honeybird, and flew off.

Leza began to climb down the immense spider's web which hung from the sky. Though its fabric was almost too fine to see, it was strong enough to bear his weight: so much of him was sunshine.

Meanwhile, the Honeybird wondered about the three calabashes round its neck: whether they contained any magic for birds, whether First Man and First Woman deserved such a gift, and whether they would be grateful. The gourds were very light to carry: had Leza even remembered to fill them?

That was Honeybird's excuse to peck a small hole in the first calabash.

Out spilled seeds and grain, hips and haws, bulbs and corms – all good things to plant in the newly made Earth. Honeybird cocked first one curious eye and then the other over the seed . . . and could see no harm in opening the second calabash.

Out spilled herbs and spices, gold-dust and ore, pollen and resin – all useful things for a life in a new young world. Honeybird turned each marvel over with its delicate claw . . . and saw no harm in opening the third calabash.

Out spilled termites and leeches, sickness and madness, weariness and disease, the roaring of a lion, the sharpness of a thorn; vipers and scorpions, misery, pain. And Death. Slithering away faster than thought, each evil thing wriggled into the cracked ground, into hollow trees, into rock crevices or in under the beds of First Man and First Woman.

'What have you done, you fool!' Leza's voice boomed out behind the Honeybird and ruffled all its feathers with the blast of his breath. 'Could you not have waited a few short moments? My people will never forgive you for this!'

He tried with all his superhuman might to recapture the wild beasts and vile evils let loose, but they were already gone, already lurking in the Earth's dark places.

With infinite care, Leza-the-Infinite explained to First Man and First Woman what to do with the seeds and bulbs and herbs, the metal and the pollen. He told them how to worship him, how to get by amid the troubles Honeybird had brought on them. Then he kissed them and climbed back up the spider's web.

But First Man and First Woman did not want to be left alone. They were so alarmed by the scrabblings under their beds, at the slitherings among their flowers, at the hoots which haunted their sleep, that they picked up their belongings and followed Leza.

'He's safe in the sky; why shouldn't we live there with him?' they reasoned. 'After all, *we* are more special than any of the *other* creatures he made. We'll be safe there!' And they began to scramble up the spider's web.

The web stretched. Its intricate pattern was pulled out of shape by their weight and the weight of all their belongings. At last, with a twang as loud as a hair breaking, the web shredded and tore and fell, tumbling First Man and First Woman back to Earth in a tangle of gossamer.

Leza was appalled at their arrogance, astonished at their presumption. 'Try and climb up to my home?' he cried. 'Is there no end to their ambition?' And he kept himself to himself after that, confined himself to his shelf of sky-blue vapour, and did not come and go between Earth and Sky as he had done before.

The Honeybird, meantime, does what it can to make amends. Whenever it comes across Man or Woman, Son or Daughter, it darts down, uttering its piercing cry of 'Follow, Follow!', leading the way to golden hoards of hidden honey, to crystalline combs of sweetness, in the hope that one day they will forgive the matter of the third calabash.

The Sky-Blue Storybox

A LEGEND FROM GHANA

B Y NOW, you have heard many stories. Forget them. Imagine you have never heard any; that there are no stories to hear. That is what the world was like when Anansi was young – when all the stories were kept in a strongbox, up in Heaven.

Everyone needs stories, not least Anansi the Spider Man. He wanted them for himself and for his family. He wanted the power that stories bring, the respect that comes to the story-teller, the taste of those stories in his mouth. So he wove a web and climbed up it to Heaven, and he said to Sky-God, 'Tell me the price of the Sky-Blue Storybox.'

'Aho,' said Sky-God. 'Many have wanted to buy my Storybox: kings and sorcerers and millionaires. But none could muster the price.'

'What is the price?' asked Anansi.

'All the spots on the leopard, a handful of hornets, a rainbow python and a fairy. Bring me all these and the stories are yours.'

Anansi bowed. 'I'll be back,' he said.

The leopard part was easy.

All he had to do was dig a pit and brew a keg of beer. Then, inviting Leopard home for a drink, he took sips, while Leopard drank deep. By the time Leopard reeled home he was in no fit state to see the pit in his path. In he fell, and with such a thud that his spots all fell off. Then Anansi brought a ladder and, with tender concern, helped Leopard out.

Later, all that remained was to gather up the spots . . .
Which left the hornets, the python and the fairy.

At this point, Anansi felt a little uneasy, for he had no
idea how to catch a handful of hornets.

'What you need,' said his wife, 'is a gourd, a leaf from a
banana tree and a cup of water.'

'I see what you mean!' said Anansi. The gourd he cut a
hole in; the leaf he put on his head. The cup of water he
threw in the air.

'Hornets! Oh, hornets!' called Anansi. 'What will become of you, now that the rains have come?'

A passing swarm of hornets looked at Anansi. The rains
surely had come. Why else would anyone be standing with
a dripping banana leaf on his head?

'Shelter in this gourd, friends, and be quick about it!'
urged Anansi, 'or the rains will smash your silver wings!'

At once the hornets flew into the gourd, thanking Anansi
as they did so. As soon as they were inside, Anansi plugged
the hole. There it was. A hand-grenade of hornets . . .
Which left only the python and the fairy.

At this point Anansi was in a bit of a quandary, for he
had no idea how to catch a rainbow python.

'What you need is a tree trunk and a length of twine,'
said his wife.

'I see that, plain as day!' said Anansi. Immediately, he
went and cut down a tall palm tree and stripped it bare.
Then, with the tree tucked under two or three arms, he
walked through the jungle, talking to it as he went. 'He is, I
tell you,' said Anansi to the tree, and then, 'I tell you he *is!*
I'll prove it to you!' and then, 'Don't argue!'

The rainbow python was puzzled (as anyone would be)
to see Anansi talking to a tree. 'Ho there, Anansi! What
gives, man?'

'My friend here,' (said Anansi to the python) 'says that
he's longer than you, but I say you're longer. Won't you
settle the argument, once and for all?'

'Of course, of course,' said the python, flattered, and lay down alongside the palm tree. Round once, round twice, round three times, Anansi bound the twine, until he reached the python's head. 'I believe,' he said, 'that now you're mine for the giving . . . Which leaves only the fairy.'

Now Anansi had not the remotest idea how to catch a fairy. His wife said, 'What you need is a wooden dolly and some sap from the gum tree.'

'Of course,' said Anansi, and then, 'Why's that?'

'To make a gum baby, of course!' said his wife.

'Of course! Of course! said Anansi. 'A gum . . . what was that?'

'And some banana mash for it to hold,' said his patient wife.

At last Anansi saw what she was driving at, and went to make a little wood carving of a child. This he covered in gum, and into one wooden hand he tied a bowl of banana mash. On the face he painted a smile. Then he propped the whole thing against a tree, and hid in the branches.

Before long a fairy came by and, seeing the figure holding out a bowl of banana mash, politely asked if she might have some.

Dolly didn't say 'Yes', didn't say 'No'; it just smiled. So the fairy helped herself. She even said, 'Thank you.'

Dolly didn't say 'Stay', didn't say 'Go'; it just smiled.

'What's your name?' asked the fairy.

Dolly didn't say 'Jess', didn't say 'Mo'; it just smiled.

'Are you deaf?' asked the fairy.

Dolly didn't say 'Guess', didn't say 'So'; it just smiled. At which the fairy started to feel seriously put out, and gave the dolly a push on the shoulder. 'Speak, can't you?'

Dolly didn't speak fast, didn't speak slow; it just smiled. But it didn't let got of the fairy's hand either, seeing as its shoulder was sticky as flypaper.

'Don't just stand there grinning!' snapped the fairy. 'Give me back my hand!' And she slapped the other shoulder. There she stuck, like a wasp in jam. She gave the dolly a kick with both feet, and butted it, too.

Dolly didn't say 'Cease', didn't say 'Ow!'; it just smiled its sticky smile, hard up against the fairy's face.

That was when Anansi climbed down out of the tree, picked up the dolly and the fairy (stuck as fast together as the two sides of a sandwich) and carried her up to Sky-God, along with the rainbow python, the gourd full of hornets and purse full of leopard spots.

Sky-God looked at the great squeaking, buzzing bundles laid down at his feet and his eyes were round as full moons. 'What's this you've brought me, Spider Man Anansi?'

'The price of the Sky-Blue Storybox, master,' said Anansi. 'The gourd is full of hornets, so be careful how you take off the lid.'

'Many have asked to buy the Storybox,' said Sky-God 'but only Spider Man Anansi has managed to pay the price, tricky devil that he is.' So saying, Sky-God laid one finger on each bundle: 'I have touched them; they are mine!' he said, trying to unstick his finger from the gummy fairy. 'The Storybox is yours, Mister Anansi!'

So Anansi climbed down his web out of the sky, the box tucked under four of his arms. And half-way down he cracked it open and began spilling out the stories: riddles and fables, parables and sagas, ballads and myths and legends.

'Wey, Spider Man!' called Sky-God. 'What you doing, man? Ain't you gonna sell them or keep them for a treasure all to yourself?'

'I know what I'm doing,' said Anansi. 'They're mine, so they're mine to let go!'

Pretty soon, Sky-God let go the rainbow python and the leopard too, the angry hornets and the fairy; they were his, so they were his to let go. Naturally, they were livid with Anansi, and went looking for him, to pay him back.

But by then, the people of Earth were so grateful to

Anansi for the stories he had spilled that they hid and harboured their hero safe and sound.

It took a while for those stories to spread world-wide, but not so long as you might think, given the size of the world. Wherever a traveller made tracks he carried a wealth of stories, to pay for his supper or a bed for the night. And that's how stories spread far and farther than far.

But answer this riddle. If there were no stories before Spider Man Anansi fetched down his prize, where did I find the story of Anansi and the Sky-Blue Storybox? . . . eh?

A Question of Arithmagic

I F ALL the villains in the world were stupid, it would not matter whether or not kings were wise. But many of the wickedest people are dangerously clever, and most cunning of all are the trolls.

Fortunately, Olaf Tryggvason was not merely a king, he was a scholar, too. He could read, write and add up; sometimes even do all three at once. The warriors who manned the oars of his ship were strong and fearless, loyal and handsome – men like Thorgeir the Bold – but they held the King in awe and admiration, because he was a scholar and a thinking man.

Sailing one day through the dank Icelandic mists of winter, King Olaf commanded his navigator to steer close by the cliffs. 'If we keep land within sight,' he said, 'we cannot lose our way in this infernal fog.' So carefully, gingerly, the dragon-prowed ship moved along the rocky coastline, close enough inshore to see gannets and cormorants riding on the updraught, close enough to see seals sleeping in the coves, sea pinks growing in the rocky crevices. They sailed so close, they even caught sight of an old man balanced precariously on a narrow shelf of rock half-way up the cliffs. The King hailed him through cupped hands.

'Are you stranded?' he called. 'Do you need help?'

'Not at all,' the old man called back in a voice clear and strong. 'Greetings, King Olaf Tryggvason. Hail and all hail.' Something about the voice made Thorgeir miss his oar-stroke.

'What's your name? Where do you live?' called the King, for it was a wild, inhospitable coast with not a house in sight.

'I live in this cliff, of course: I and all my fighting men.'

King Olaf was intrigued. He knew nothing of any warlord living in this part of his kingdom, nor of any army, although he made it his business to know such things. 'And how many men do you command, sir?'

The old man began to chant:

> 'Twelve ships have I with oaken keels;
> In every boat there ride twelve crew.
> Each rower kills a dozen seals,
> To make our daily meal of stew,
> And cuts each skin in twelve and then
> Each strip is cut in twelve again;
> Each portion cut must serve ten men:
> How many are my followers, then?'

The King laughed and clapped his hands. A riddle! There was nothing he liked better. Calling for paper, he began to work the problem out. 'Twelve ships and each one has twelve . . . that's one hundred and forty-four rowers . . .' The King sucked the feather of his pen and frowned as he struggled with the mathematics.

Thorgeir, meantime, noticed a certain side-slipping motion of the ship. The birds of the cliff seemed bigger than before.

'One hundred and forty-four rowers kill twelve seals each: that's . . . one seven two eight . . .' The King's quill scratched busily.

Thorgeir, meantime, stood up to get a proper look at the old man on the cliff. He seemed to be chanting under his breath. More poetry, perhaps? Or there again, perhaps not.

'One thousand, seven hundred and twenty-eight seal-skins, all cut into twelve,' mused the King. 'That's four, carry one – eight – one, carry one . . . By the gods, this man has a bigger army than I do . . . !'

Thorgeir, meantime, felt a faint grating on the ship's hull. It was being pulled steadily inshore, closer and closer to the snarling rocks. As a whirlpool sucks ships into its swilly mouth, the old man's chanting was dragging the King's ship to its destruction. 'Your Majesty . . .' he began.

'Don't interrupt, I'm multiplying,' muttered King Olaf, and went on counting imaginary strips of sealskin.

The old man was clearly visible now, much closer than before. Thorgeir could see how his yellow eyes glinted and his snaggled teeth were bared in an evil grin. The oarsman pulled his oar out of the rowlock, but it was too short for the job. He cut through the sheets of the mainsail and heaved the mast itself out of its socket in the deck. Resting it on the ship's rail, he put his chest against its end and prepared for a jarring shock.

'. . . and if each portion feeds ten men . . .' muttered the King.

'I think, master, that this old man . . .' grunted Thorgeir, struggling with the weight of the mast.

'You'll make me lose my place,' said the King, bending over his sums.

Then the tip of the mast struck the cliff with a force which broke three of Thorgeir's ribs. Still he strained to hold the ship away from the cliff which would rip out its side.

The old man on the cliff, seeing Thorgeir's efforts, scowled at him and chanted faster and louder, a magic chant, a troll chant to wreck the King of Iceland. He cursed Thorgeir, with all the black arts of trolldom.

The magic dragged on the ship as though the very cliff were a magnet and the ship a twopenny plug of iron. Thorgeir felt his breastbone bend, his heart falter within him, but still he held the ship off the cliff.

'So I make that fifty-one thousand, eight-hundred

and . . .' said King Olaf Tryggvason. But his answer was never finished. With a noise like a lightning-strike, the mast snapped as, with one final mighty effort, Thorgeir levered the dragon-prowed ship out into deeper water. That great jerking thrust was enough to break the power of the old man's magic. He had to watch his prize escape him, pitching and rolling out of harm's way.

The King lost his footing and fell on his back, ink spilling over the workings of his sum. Looking up, he was in time to see the old man on the cliff change back into his rightful shape – three coils of a hideous nose, and a face like mouldy cheese. 'By the gods, it was a troll!' – he cried. 'D'you see that, Thorgeir? It was a troll trying to lure us on to the rocks!'

Thorgeir said nothing, but lay in the bottom of the boat, content to have saved the King and his comrades from a miserable death on the rocks. 'It is a wonderful thing,' he consoled himself, 'to have a scholar for a king.'

But a bit of common sense doesn't go amiss, either.

The Alchemist

A CHINESE LEGEND

MR CHIA was a laundryman. All day he beat the soapy washing clean on a huge block of stone using a long wooden bat: a tedious, wearisome job. But he passed the time thinking about money and what he would do with it if he ever had any.

One day he saw a cart offloading furniture at a house nearby. Chia went at once to call on his new neighbour – his new and *affluent*-looking neighbour – to introduce himself. But the gentleman seemed always to be out. In the end, Chia resorted to hiding in a bush and jumping out as the man put his key in the door. Then he bowed politely and presented a bottle of wine: 'A gift of welcome from your humble neighbour,' he said.

'Charmed, charmed,' said the gentleman. 'Come indoors and let us share this wine! My name is Chên.'

It was a hot day. The wine slipped down deliciously, and the two got on well. There seemed nothing exceptional about Mr Chên except perhaps his good looks and musical speaking voice. When the wine was almost gone, he fetched a large jade jug and poured the last drop into it.

At once the jug filled to the brim with the best wine Chia had ever tasted. 'What a trick!' he gasped. 'Can you do any more?'

Chên smiled benignly and took out a small shiny black stone. He spoke a few words, rubbed the stone against a vase – and at once the vase turned to silver.

—— 171 ——

Chia gasped. 'Where did you get that stone? What is it? I want one! Where can I get one? Where?'

Mr Chên sighed. 'I was afraid of this. I was told in Heaven that you are a greedy man, Mr Chia.'

'Greedy? Me?'

'That's why I tried to avoid meeting you. You must understand: we Immortals are not permitted to teach alchemy to you mortals. Imagine the chaos it could cause here on Earth.'

'Oh, absolutely. Chaos! I quite understand!' said Chia. 'Have another drink.'

Twenty drinks later, as Chên slithered like a pickled eel out of his armchair and on to the floor, Chia searched his robe, found the lodestone, let himself out and went home.

It was no use, of course. He did not know the magic words, and so, although he rubbed pots, bottles, cups, melons and the dog, his alchemy simply did not work.

It was some hours before Mr Chên woke up. When he realized his lodestone was missing, he assumed he had lost it by sheer carelessness, and scoured the house, the garden, the street – even went over to the laundry to tell his neighbour of the disaster.

But Chia greeted him with good news as he opened the door: 'Ah! My friend! I found something of yours this morning!'

'My lodestone?'

'Your lodestone, yes! In the street! You must have dropped it.'

Mr Chên was overjoyed. 'How can I ever thank you! I should be in such trouble in Heaven if they found out I'd lost it!'

Chia bowed. 'Don't mention it . . . only I suppose you might see fit to reward me by letting me use the stone. Just once!'

Chên was flustered. 'Impossible! I mustn't! It's forbid-den!' But Chia looked so hurt, made Chên feel so ungrateful and mean, that finally he agreed. 'I'll show you – but you must *promise* not to be greedy. Change a few lead coins perhaps, or a pebble. Otherwise the gods are bound to find out what I've done.'

'Something like this, say?' said Chia, holding up a bar of soap.

Chên mopped his brow with relief. 'Clearly the rumours I heard about you in Heaven were quite ill-founded!'

Chia put the tiny morsel of soap on the huge wash-slab where every day he beat the washing clean.

'Now say:

> 'As Earth is to Heaven, as little is to much,
> Lodestone raise the nature of whate'er you touch.'

Chia's fingers, clutching the shiny black stone, hovered for a moment over the sliver of soap as he spoke the magic words . . . Then they dodged aside and quickly rubbed the wash-block. Instantly, half a ton of silver stood gleaming amid the laundry.

'No! *No!* What have you done?' cried Chên. 'My name will be struck from the Book of Angels for this! How could you! What will become of me? No! No!' He rushed out of the laundry tearing his hair and reproaching Chia bitterly for his deceitful trick. But Chia hardly heard. He was busy staring at his reflection in the shining silver slab.

A year went by. One day, an elegant gentleman arrived in town and knocked at the laundry door, asking for Chia. But Mr Chia was out: 'At the hospital, probably,' he was told.

He was on his way there when he met Chia coming the other way. The two recognized each other at once.

'My dear Chia!'

'My dear Chên! How have you been, all this time?'

'Not bad! Of course, at first my name was struck from

the Book of Angels, as I said it would be. The gods were furious with me for sharing the secret of alchemy. But after you built the new school and all those houses for the poor, and the hospital, the monastery – those orphanages, and planted all those blossom trees . . . Well, I was summoned to Heaven. "We misjudged you, Mr Chên!" they said. "Through this man, you have done more good on Earth than we have managed in many a year . . ." I must admit, though: for a time *I* misjudged *you*, my dear Chia.'

'What? You didn't really think I'd spend all that silver on myself? With so much poverty all around me? I used to dream, while I beat those clothes, how I'd wash away a thousand miseries if I ever had the money. And you, my friend, you gave me the opportunity.'

So they shared a bottle of wine, and parted. 'Until we meet again in Heaven!' said Mr Chên.

'You really think there's place in Heaven for a poor laundryman like me?' exclaimed Mr Chia delightedly. 'Ah well, yes, I suppose the angels need their clothes washed just like everyone else. Till we meet, then in Heaven's laundry!'

Workshy Rabbit

A WEST AFRICAN LEGEND

THEY SAY that rabbits hate hard work, but that's a filthy slur on rabbits. I know of one who put himself to infinite pains, took tremendous trouble, expended endless energy on a project . . . even if it was to get out of working. Of course, it happened long ago – before most animals had ever met, and before they knew how each other looked. Only Rabbit, who scurried about seeing all that was to be seen and getting what was to be got, knew that here lived wildebeest and there a tortoise, here a lion and there a jackal, here an elephant and there a giraffe.

The corn needed planting, so Rabbit went to Elephant and said, 'We animals should help one another. If you'll push down the trees to clear the ground, I will burn them.' Elephant agreed at once, and spent all day barging trees out of the ground with his massive head. It was hard work: he was not the biggest of his breed.

Meanwhile, Rabbit went to Giraffe and said, 'I've done all the hard work rooting out the trees. If you burn off the timber, we can plant as soon as the rains come. We animals should cooperate, don't you agree?' Giraffe agreed. She burned off the fallen timber, amazed that little Rabbit had been able to flatten so many trees single-handedly.

The rains came in like blades of silver slicing through the heat and drenching the ashy earth of the clearing. Rabbit went to Elephant and said, 'If you do the sowing, I'll do the hoeing.' Which Elephant did.

Then Rabbit went to Giraffe and said, 'I've done the sowing. It's your turn to do the hoeing.' Which Giraffe did.

The corn grew tall and golden. When it was ripe, Rabbit went to Elephant and said, 'You reap and afterwards I'll gather . . . Oh, but look out for an animal called Giraffe. I hear she's a terrible thief of ripe corn.' Elephant slashed down the corn with scything sweeps of his long tusks, but of Giraffe he saw not a nose nor a neck.

Meanwhile, Rabbit went to Giraffe and said, 'I've reaped the corn. Time for you to gather up the cobs . . . But do look out for that thieving beast called Elephant; he'd steal the corn from his own granny.' Giraffe gathered up the corn cobs into a pile almost as high as her head, but of Elephant she saw not a tail nor a trunk.

Rabbit sat by and watched, just working up an appetite. 'Reckon that Elephant is bound to come sniffing round tomorrow, wanting to steal our corn,' he called out to Giraffe.

'He'll be sorry if he does,' said Giraffe, stamping all four elegant feet in turn.

Before going to bed, Rabbit called on Elephant, too, and said, 'Reckon that Giraffe may come filching our corn one day soon.'

'She'll regret it if she does!' snorted Elephant.

Now the plan was that Rabbit would get up early next day and help himself to as much corn as he wanted before the others arrived. They would simply blame each other for the theft.

But Rabbit overslept: he had quite worn himself out with all that to-ing and fro-ing and mischief-making. When he got to the field, Giraffe was already there. Rabbit thought once and thought again.

'Oh! Look out! Here comes that thieving Elephant to help himself to our corn!' he cried.

'Where? Where?' said Giraffe, baring her teeth and bridling.

'There! There!' said Rabbit, pointing to a mountain.

'Over that mountain?' said Giraffe.

'What mountain?' said Rabbit. 'That IS Elephant!'

At that Giraffe's long legs bowed and her neck sagged and her ears hung down like yellow banana peel. 'God help us! We can't fight a monster like that!' she cried, and promptly fainted clean away.

Rabbit took the opportunity to nibble a breakfast of corn, tossing the chewed husks all around. Before long, around the mountain and down the road came Elephant – not the biggest of his kind – looking all around him for corn thieves. 'Seen any sign of that Giraffe?' he asked Rabbit, and Rabbit nodded furiously.

'Yes! She was here just now! See where she made a start on our corn! She said it was so sweet she'd fetch her mate, and together they would polish off the lot!'

'Cheek! Didn't you chase her away, the impudent whippersnapper?' asked Elephant, outraged.

Rabbit wiffled his nose and trembled his ears and looked as timid as any . . . well, as any rabbit. 'Who me? Tackle a brute like that? Giant Giraffe?'

'Why? Is she very big?' snorted Elephant, contemptuous and swaggering. 'Not too big for *me* to handle, I'll bet!'

Rabbit spread his paws wide, seeming to search for some way of describing the enormity of Giraffe. 'Well, look, that's her guitar lying on the ground,' he said, pointing at the sprawling Giraffe. 'That will give you some idea how big she is.'

At that, Elephant folded his ears on top of his head, picked up his big feet and took off at a run. 'That's her guitar. In that case I'm getting out of here before she uses me for a bongo!'

As soon as Giraffe came round, she too hurried to make her excuses and leave. 'Never really liked corn much anyway,' she said. 'You have it, Rabbit. You eat what you can before that Elephant gets here. Look at the size of him! Big as a hill! Big as a mountain, almost! I'm off!' And away she ran, stretching out her long neck for all the world like the fretboard of the world's largest guitar.

So Rabbit had plenty of time to eat his crop of corn, all the time in the world to laze in the sun and figure out why God made Elephant so big and Giraffe so tall . . . but gave all the brains to rabbits.

Cat v. Rat

THERE was a time, before times changed, when Cat and Rat got along pretty well. They got on like the best of friends, because that's what they were. They lived on an island so far out to sea that the mainland was only a rim of dark along the horizon, and Cat ate the birds out of the trees and Rat ate the roots of the cassava trees.

Still, there was only one kind of bird on the island, and cassava is cassava, call it manioc or tapioca or what you will. Both Cat and Rat craved variety.

'I bet there's all kinds of food out there,' said Rat, pointing with her stringy tail over the sea.

'As many different birds as there are stars,' agreed Cat gloomily, 'but not for us.'

'We could always go there,' said Rat, but Cat's fur stood on end at the thought of all that water.

'I can't swim.'

'You never tried. Anyway, we could make a boat.'

'My dear old furless friend,' gasped Cat, 'what a genius you are!'

Together they dug up a tough old cassava root and, while Cat scraped off the dirt outside, Rat gnawed out a hollow, eating the white pulpy strands as she went. 'When I get to the mainland,' she said, her little belly bulging. 'I never want to see another cassava.'

Now it so happens that cassava juice is a powerful strong drink, and by the time the canoe was finished, the two animals were singing slurred songs, trying to dance and stand on their heads and juggle crabs and so forth. They just leapt aboard and paddled excitedly out to sea.

It was much further than it looked to the mainland.

Paddling was hot, hungry work. When they stopped, the canoe stopped too. It looked as though the journey might take days.

'We forgot to bring any food,' said Rat.

'At least you ate before we set out. All that cassava,' said Cat. 'I'm hungry.'

'Go to sleep. You won't notice then,' said Rat, and they both curled up in the circle of their tails, at either end of the boat, and tried to sleep. Cat was soon dreaming of birds, his paws making little pat-patting movements in his sleep. But Rat could not sleep. A few hours before, she had never wanted to see another cassava root. Now a little cassava sounded very appetizing. 'And if I just scoop out a little more of the canoe, Cat will never know.'

She scooped and nibbled, nibbled and scooped the cassava canoe hollower than before. But not enough for Cat to notice.

Next night, while Cat slept, Rat scooped and nibbled a little more. Scoop, nibble, nibble, scoop. Whoops. One scoop too many.

It spurted a fountain of seawater. The sleeping Cat felt a sudden coldness around the tail area, and woke up to find the boat awash.

'You greedy guts! You peabrain gobbling twiddler! You've chewed through the bottom of the boat! Argghh! I hate water! I ought to eat you here and now, you treacherous little scrabbler!'

'Quite right, quite right!' squealed Rat, paddling furiously while the water came up around her haunches. 'I'll just help you get ashore, and then you really must eat me up from head to tail.'

So Cat paddled, too, though by the time they reached the mainland shore, they were up to their necks in the briny, and their canoe was entirely swamped. 'Just wait till I get my claws on you,' hissed Cat, crawling up the beach. He did not know whether anger or hunger made him keenest to eat Rat.

'Oh, your lovely fur!' cried Rat. 'Don't let it dry with all that salt in it! Poor dear Cat! Don't catch cold! Get dry, do! Groom yourself! I couldn't bear it if you caught pneumonia on my account.'

So Cat sat and licked his salty coat till it was dry and shining, savouring the moment when he would bite off Rat's head.

But when he looked round, all that he found was a small hole dug in the beach. 'Rat? Are you down there?'

'Mmmm,' said Rat. 'I have to admit I am.'

'Then come out at once and let me eat you.'

'We-e-ll. Perhaps not just yet,' said Rat.

'I can wait,' said Cat. 'You have to come out some time.'

'I'll just prepare myself for death, then, and be out directly,' said Rat.

So while Cat sat guard at the entry to the hole, Rat dug deeper and deeper – a longer and longer tunnel which broke surface under the shadow of the trees. Rat slunk off, snickering.

For three days Cat sat and waited for Rat to give herself up, before realizing that he had been duped once again. He swore then a vengeance so terrible that the palm trees shook, and rained down coconuts on his head.

So now the hunt is really on. From town to town, country to country, Cat hunts Rat, determined to kill that perfidious, cheating, no-good, scrabbling rodent. Generations of cats have taught their kittens to hate and hunt the whole ratty breed. And wherever there's a hole with a rattish sort of shape to it, you will find a cat waiting his chance to pounce . . .

The Pied Piper

A GERMAN LEGEND

ONE DAY Frau Fogel put her hand into the bread bin, and something brushed against it, warm and furry, which sank its teeth into her palm and drew blood.

Next door, Frau Reuzel went to kiss her baby, and found something grey and sleek curled up against the baby's cheek, the cot full of droppings.

At the inn, the innkeeper opened his cellar doors and was met by a flood of fur, a sea of rats, which washed over his feet and streamed away into every corner, squealing.

The little town of Hamelin was infested with rats. Not a house was free of them, not a corner safe to set down a child or a plate of food. Rats moved along the Mayor's white tablecloth, even while the Mayor ate his dinner. Evil, filthy, beady-eyed, with tails like earthworms and teeth like needles, they no longer ran away from the brooms which tried to sweep them out-of-doors, but chewed on the broom bristles and swarmed where they passed.

'Get rid of them! Please!' pleaded the people, banging on the Mayor's door. 'Do something, or what do we pay taxes for?'

'I sent the public rat-catcher, didn't I? With his bucket and pole,' said the Mayor from an upstairs window. 'What more do you want?'

'But the rats ate him!'

'And his bucket!'

'And his pole!'

'*Do something!*'

It was at this moment that a stranger arrived in town. He attracted stares, but no friendly greeting, for he was an odd-looking creature in parti-coloured clothes like a jester – one stocking green, one red, one sleeve blue, one yellow. He wore his hair long, slicked down against his head and shoulders, and a jacket with long tapering tails right down to his dusty boots. He played a pipe, too, and Hamelin was not accustomed to music; the people there had never yet discovered what purpose it served, what profit was to be made from it.

The children liked him, of course, but then children are notoriously bad judges of character. They like a person because he makes them laugh, and ignore a man with ten thousand in the bank. In the town square, the stranger raised his pointed nose in the air and cocked his head, as if those small round ears so high up on his head could hear something out of the ordinary.

'What d'you want?' shouted the town beadle. 'Keep right on going. We have rodents enough round here already.'

'Perhaps I can help you, then . . .' said the stranger.

He said that he could rid the town of rats. For one hundred gold pieces, he would drown them in the river and end the plague.

'Give him the money! Give it!' shouted the crowd gathered outside the Mayor's house. 'Pay the Piper!'

'Anyone can make grand promises,' said the Mayor. 'But can he keep them? First let him do it, and then I'll pay!' From the eaves and sills, crouched on shop signs and along the rim of the ornamental fountain, a million rats looked on with glittering eyes.

'A hundred pieces of gold when I've rid you of rats,' said the stranger. And the Mayor blustered, 'Yes, yes.'

So the Piper put his pipe to his lips and played a tune. It

had four beats to the bar, because rats go on four feet. It had a bleak, grey, scampering squeal which set everyone's teeth on edge. But the rats loved it.

The rats were spellbound by it. Captivated. Out of the houses and drains, the gutters and lofts and cellars, out of the cradles and cupboards, the breadbins and rubbish, the water butts and covered carts, a tide of grey vermin swirled down towards the playing of the pipe. Men and women alike screamed at the sheer number – they had never realized! – old men fainted at the stench. But the Piper just went on playing, strolling down towards the bridge, towards the river.

He sank them in the river: he played them to their deaths. Rafts of rats floated down the Weser River, their tails trailing like so many extinguished candle wicks. A strange silence replaced the ceaseless whistle of rodents squealing, the ceaseless scrabble of their claws. There was only the pleasant sound of children playing. Nothing but the rats' droppings and their teethmarks in the cheese remained to prove they had ever been there. And those were soon cleared away.

'What rats!' said the Mayor when the Piper asked for his money. 'I see no rats. I recall no rats.'

'You promised me one hundred gold pieces.'

'Promised? I remember no promise.'

The Piper turned towards the stallholders in the market-place. He was wearing black and white now – pied like the thieving magpie – though no one had seen him change his clothes, or could see where he had carried such baggage. They heard his argument with the Mayor, but they said nothing. After all, the hundred gold pieces would have been paid out of *their* taxes.

'Pay him!' said a child. But then children have no sense of business. They would squander money on anything.

Then the Pied Piper put his pipe to his lips and played another tune. For a man cheated out of money it was a remarkably cheerful tune – a dance, a caper full of laughing trills. And it had *two* beats to the bar.

The children loved it. The children were captivated by it. Enchanted. Throughout Hamelin they left their desks, their toys, their books and games. The older ones picked up their baby brothers and sisters and carried them. They walked and skipped and danced and toddled down towards the bridge and over the river.

Their parents were busy – so much to do now that the rats had gone. They did not realize what was happening. A strange silence replaced the crying of babies, the chant of children playing or reciting their lessons. It was not until the schoolmaster stood at his school gate, screaming himself blue, that the parents noticed their children – all their children – topping a rise on the mountain road, following the Pied Piper. Following, following. Leaving, leaving, leaving them behind.

How those mothers and fathers ran and called and hallooed. Shoes sliding in the dirt, aprons clenched in fists, shouting children's names, shouting promises: 'We'll pay you! A hundred gold pieces! A *thousand* gold pieces! *Come back!*'

The Koppenberg Hill resounded with their shouts, shook with them. It fractured and tore itself apart, opening a rift in the rocks as great as a cathedral door. In at the door went the Pied Piper and behind him the children, without a backward glance. The hill healed itself, closed and knit so completely that no trace remained of the door by the time mothers started clawing at it with their bare hands. '*Don't go! Come back!*'

The human heart does not mend so easily as rock, and that day every heart in Hamelin was broken.

'It's your fault they're gone! You should have paid him!' they shouted, beating on the Mayor's door. 'Where are our children!'

'Children? What children?' said the Mayor in terror.

'You have no children now. Forget them! They're gone. What purpose did they serve, in any case? What are they good for – babies, children? I never understood. Work! Profit! They're the only things that really matter! That's all we have to worry ourselves about now. Work! Profit! And —'

'*Death!*' cried the people of Hamelin as they stormed the Mayor's house like a pack of ravenous rats.

Gull-Girl

A LEGEND FROM SIBERIA

T HE DAY was so hot that the cats took off their fur, the seals their skins and even Gregor took off his jacket. The fish gaped for air in the tepid lake, and a flock of geese and gulls floated overhead like ash over a bonfire. If it had not been for his mother's nagging, Gregor would never have bothered to go hunting on a day like this.

Idly, he watched the birds sweep in to land on the bank of the lake, watched them strip off their white feather cloaks, watched the goosemaidens and gull-girls inside wade into the water and swim. Quick as a whistle, Gregor ran and snatched up as many cloaks as his arms could carry.

'Oh, no! Thief! Give them back!' came the raucous cries from the lake. 'Don't take our feathers from us, or how shall we fly?' White arms reached out to him; white hands implored him. And Gregor did give back his trophies, cloak by beautiful cloak. All except one. One of the gull-girls was beautiful. Gregor could not bear to let her go.

'You're mine,' he said to the gull-girl.

'I'm promised to the Chief of the Sea Birds!' protested Gull-girl. But Gregor took her promise and broke it, for he was too much in love to care.

Gregor was not a bad man. This one unkindness was the first and last in his life. Gull-girl Chaika had no complaints after she married him, and they came by two pretty children as well as a big feather bed.

Life was as sweet as a melon. But every melon has pips

and, as it happened, Gregor's mother was about as pleasant as a whole mouthful of pips.

'Call that a pie?' she would say, when Chaika cooked. 'I've thrown tastier logs on the fire!'

'Call that clean?' she would say, when Chaika tidied the house. 'I've seen pigs keep their sties cleaner.'

'Call that washed?' she would say, when Chaika did the laundry. 'I've seen scarecrows better dressed than my son since you married him!' On and on she nagged. 'You, you haven't wits enough to stuff a cushion! I knew my Gregor was stupid, but I never knew he was stupid enough to marry a dumb-cluck chicken!'

Chaika bore it until she could bear it no longer. One day, when she was alone at home with the children, she slit open the feather bed with a knife, stuck feathers to the arms and shoulders of her son and daughter, and flew away with them to the Land of Birds. Gregor heard her shrill gull-squawk of farewell as she swooped overhead, then away and away.

'Good riddance,' said his mother, but Gregor stamped his boot.

'This is all your doing! So you can just sit down and sew me ten pairs of boots. When they're made, I'll search the world till I've found Chaika and the children and brought them home again!'

He was as good as his word. With nine pairs of boots in a sack over his shoulder, he set off to search the world. High summer turned to deepest winter, and one by one he wore out the boots in searching.

He had just laced on the ninth pair when he reached the mountain-top eyrie of a golden eagle. There he bowed down low in respect and said, 'Mighty King of the Birds, I married a gull-girl, but she has flown away and left me. Help me to find her and my two children.'

Golden Eagle was astounded at Gregor's courage. 'Don't you realize I could tear out your heart with my beak, or carry you into the air in my claws and drop you from top to bottom of this mountain of mine?'

'Without Chaika and my little chickabiddy children, I don't much care if you do,' said Gregor forlornly.

So the eagle took pity on him and sent him down to the seashore – a long journey from a mountain top. 'Go down to the sea and see what you can see,' said Golden Eagle.

Gregor had just laced on his last pair of boots when he reached the seashore and saw an old carpenter building a boat down by the sea.

'Can you tell me the way to Bird Land?' he asked.

'What will you pay for my answer?' replied the carpenter.

'Sir, I've nothing left in the world but one pair of boots.'

'They'll do,' said the giant looking him over, and he ran his plane one last time along the curve of a newly made canoe, struck his chisel against the carvings on its prow. 'This canoe will take you there,' he said, sliding open the wooden bow-cover – a bark lid carved with miraculous beasts and birds, letters and numbers, signs, symbols and mysteries.

Gregor helped him carry the boat down to the water, climbed in and sailed away. He had only to speak his wishes and the magic canoe sped over the water, so he asked it to take him to the Land of Birds, and who should he see when land came in sight, but his own two children playing on the beach.

'Daddy! Daddy!' they cried, flinging their arms round his legs.

'Where's your mother?' asked Gregor.

'Albatross, Chief of the Sea Birds, has claimed her for his own!' said the children. 'Oh, don't cross him, Daddy! He's powerful strong!'

But Gregor spat on his fists and marched right up to Chief Albatross's tent and flattened it with a single blow. When the big white bird came fluttering out, the two of them tussled and wrestled from one day's end to the next until at last Albatross, looking as scruffy as a half-plucked chicken, flapped away into the chilly sky with a dismal mewing.

Gregor kissed his wife and felt altogether pleased with himself. But Albatross had only gone to stir up the people of Bird Land.

All of a sudden, the sky turned dark with bird-wings, the wintry sun eclipsed by flocks of sharp-beaked ravens and crows and rooks. They plucked the feathers from their own wings and threw them at Gregor like black darts. But he shielded his family with the canvas from the tent, and fought back with stones and tent pegs and pieces of driftwood.

The crows and ravens and rooks fell back – only to be replaced by flocks of kites and buzzards and hawks as densely packed as swarms of gnats. All of the eastern sky was black with them, the morning light blotted out.

'We're done for now, my foolish hero,' said Chaika, and a freezing wind gave an ominous moan: *Hoowoo hoowoo!*

'Not if I have my way,' panted Gregor. 'Fetch me a bucket of fresh water and a mop.'

As though he were about to paint the heavens a better blue, Gregor soaked the mop in the water and wagged it at the sky. The water drops fell as sparkling diamonds on to the wings and backs of the flying battalions . . .

. . . and the wind froze that water into flakes of ice!

Weighed down by their little cloaks of ice, the birds fell from the sky like stones. Stalling in flight, their wings failed them. Freezing in flight, they plummeted down and lay about in thousands, winded, on the chilly ground. They were powerless to stop Gregor or his wife or his children climbing aboard the magic canoe, and long before the bird army had shaken the ice off their wings, the canoe sailed over the horizon, homeward bound.

Exhausted, the little family reached the beach where the

carpenter still stood planing boat keels. In exchange for the magic canoe, he returned Gregor's last pair of boots . . . hardly enough for the immense journey which lay ahead of them.

'Look out! They've come after us!' cried Chaika, as giant wings over-shadowed them. But it was only the golden eagle Gregor had visited on the mountain top.

'Here, borrow my cloak,' said the eagle, stepping out of his feathers. 'I want it back, mind! Flying was never meant for the human breed.'

Gratefully, Gregor pulled on the feathery pinions of the naked eagle and, tucking his family under his wings, flew as straight as an arrow, home through the sky. What a feeling that was! What a sympathy it gave him for the dipping, diving, soaring, swooping creatures he had watched so many times in the past! Gregor vowed never again to hunt wild birds, or to cage songbirds for the sake of their music.

His mother, meanwhile, having no one to nag, had found herself a husband and left Gregor's little cottage altogether. So Chaika agreed to stay, never more to put on feathers, never again to fly away. And that night, the eagle robe, lying discarded by the cottage door, flew back to its owner who was swimming luxuriously in the waters of a warm spring lake.

Arion and the Dolphins

A GREEK MYTH

K ING PERIANDER had music in his soul. That is to say there were pleasant, melodious strains and, deep down under that, a dark, reverberating bass. Just below his cultivated surface lay a temper like a shark. He was light and dark, soft and loud, generosity itself and utterly unforgiving. He surrounded himself with artists, poets, musicians; also soldiers, torturers, hangmen.

Most prized of all his friends was Arion the poet, the musician, the genius. Arion could, in playing the cithara, pluck the very heartstrings of his audience. And while he played, he sang – words of his own invention, spare and sonorous and sublime. No one who heard him could hold back either their tears or their smiles. Even the birds fell silent to listen; even the wild animals left off hunting to listen, ears cocked, eyes closed, entranced.

Arion was a quiet man, and would never have put himself forward. But Periander wanted the world to know that his court contained the very best of talents. So when he heard tell of an arts festival in Sicily, he sent Arion – 'No arguments now!' – to compete for its prizes. 'For the honour of Corinth!' he declared, so that Arion could hardly refuse.

He entered everything . . . and won, of course; trophies and laurels, chalices and purses of gold. To his shy embarrassment, he was carried through the streets shoulder-high, while young women threw flowers at him and young men begged to study at his feet. He was chaired down to the harbour and carried aboard ship: a Corinthian ship bound for its home port. 'Now take great care of Arion!' the crowd told the sailors. 'He has won every single prize at the festival. *Every single prize!*'

Now it would be wrong to impugn the honesty of Corinthian sailors, but there was a saying in those days: shake hands with them, but count your fingers afterwards. When they saw the prizes they welcomed Arion aboard. But five miles out to sea, they tipped him out of his hammock and put a dagger to his throat. 'Sorry, harp-plucker, but it's time for you to go swimming!'

Arion was not ashamed to beg for his life. 'Take the prizes; I don't want them! Just let me live!'

'Ah, but then you might say who took them,' said the Corinthian Captain, in a rasping, piratical way, trying on a golden laurel wreath. 'Whereas dead men tell no tales. Heave him over, lads.'

'I'll sing for you! I'll scrub the decks! Anything! Only don't kill me!' His back was against the ship's rail now, their hands under his armpits.

'Sing for the fishes,' said the Captain, and turned his back.

'One last song!' cried Arion. 'Let me offer up a song to the gods. Then maybe they'll pity my soul, if you won't pity my body!'

The Captain was against the idea. But the sailors could see no harm in letting Arion play, before they flung him overboard. So his beloved cithara was laid in his arms once more, and he began to sing – a wild, Corinthian lament fit to break the granite hearts of mountains.

The waves curled with pleasure at the sound. The sails, stretched taut as drumskins, throbbed with ecstasy. Fish, like a million sequins, glinted on the surface of the sea, drinking in the liquid strains of Arion's song. Seagulls perched along the yards, flightless with wonder.

Unfortunately, the sailors' idea of music was a rollicking

sea-shanty. They could beat out a jig or obey a ship's whistle, but as for Corinthian laments . . . 'Very nice, I'm sure, if you like that kind of thing,' sneered the Captain. 'Now throw him over.' Their hearts were as hard as the wax in their ears. They dropped Arion into the sea like an anchor, and he sank as though he were made of lead.

Down and down he went through a green silent world where no music sounds but the song of the whale. Though his mouth was open, no music came from it – only a stream of silver bubbles – minims of silence in a green auditorium.

Then something brushed the playing-fingers of his hand – as gently as the strings of a cithara. And a second later, a great grey flank slammed into his ribcage and another drove between his legs. He lost consciousness thinking he was being eaten by sharks.

When he opened his eyes again, the sea was a black dazzle of sunlight and his fingers were trailing through white foam. He was astride a dolphin, his face resting on a grey back as smooth as polished marble. In elegant lunges the dolphin leapt through the water, now swimming, now flying, scarcely even wetting Arion's face. Alongside swam a dozen more, leaping and plunging, chanting their strange, clicking, whistled language.

Ravished by the music coming from the ship, the dolphins had gathered round the hull to listen. Then, as the musician plunged to his supposed death, they had caught him and carried him – like the Sicilian crowds – shoulder-high across the lapis sea.

Venturing as far ashore as they dared, the dolphins dropped Arion in shallow water, then saluted him with crackling whistles before turning back out to sea. From a nearby port, Arion took ship for Corinth and was ashore before the Corinthian ship even crossed the harbour bar, telling his whole story to Periander.

They were startled to see King Periander, mighty tyrant of Corinth, standing watching them disembark. 'I was waiting for a friend,' he told them. 'Arion the poet. I thought he might have come home on your vessel.'

'Who? Ooh no,' said the Captain. 'No passengers this voyage. Arion? Sounds familiar. I recall someone of that name in Sicily. Won all the prizes at the festival. Liked the place so much he decided to stay.'

'Is that right?' said Periander mildly. 'How I'll miss his singing. I shall just have to think of some other form of entertainment.'

Suddenly the harbour was full of soldiers, their hands full of swords, ropes and chains, their mouths full of curses. The sailors offered to sing in return for their lives, to row galleys, to dive for pearls. But Periander was as deaf to their entreaties as if his ears had been full of wax. They had stirred up the blackest mud from the seabed of his soul and, by the time it settled, those Corinthian pirates wished they had never been born.

Arion did not watch. His mind was on dolphins, on the poetry and music of dolphins, on the sun-spangled sea and the sweetness of life, and on washing the sea salt out of his hair.

Thunder and Smith

A CHINESE MYTH

G ENERALLY, when people say they don't like thunder, they mean that it scares them. Not Smith. His dislike was personal. He hated Thunder with the same seething, unreasonable loathing that a man feels for a noisy neighbour. And it was mutual. Thunder would come round from time to time and beat on Smith's roof with his axe, while Smith shouted abuse at him up the chimney, and Smith's little daughter and son sat in the corner crying, 'Please don't, Daddy! Please don't! Couldn't you make things up with him and be friends?' Their father took no notice.

One day, Smith made a cage – an iron cage too big to fit through the front door – and a long iron pitchfork. He left the cage outside in the garden, camouflaged by leaves, then he sat himself down in a chair by the front door, fork in hand. He waited, waited and waited for the hot weather to break, watched the rainclouds fill up with dark rain, heard the distant grumbling of Thunder as he dragged his axe about the heavens. And he waited, still and patient, until Thunder's temper finally broke in the heat and he came rampaging over the countryside, splintering trees, knocking down chimneypots, swinging his axe like a hooligan.

Smith was ready for him. He put his thumbs in his ears and wriggled his fingers at Thunder, sticking out his tongue. When the god made a lunge at him, he jumped aside and, catching Thunder off-balance, bundled him into the cage with the fork.

'Aha! Eehee! Yahoo! Yippee!' Hopping round the cage, whooping and yelping with glee, Smith poked and jabbed through the bars. 'Got you now, you old rogue! Tee-hee! Got you, and now I'm going to cook you and eat you, braised with dumplings!'

Thunder rattled at the bars, and chewed on the lock with his yellow zigzag teeth, but because the cage was iron, he could not break free.

Little Nuwa and her brother, cowering in the doorway, hand in hand, stared and trembled. 'Oh, please, Papa! Let him go!' begged Nuwa.

But Smith was busy saddling his horse. 'I'm going to town to buy herbs – cloves and cinnamon and cardamom. I like my meat tender and tasty. You'll be quite safe: he can't get out. Just don't listen to any of his wheedling lies and you'll be fine.' And away he went, down the road, at the gallop.

He was no sooner gone than Thunder trained his steely eyes on the children and began to shout at them, 'Let me out!'

Nuwa covered her ears and told her little brother to go inside and lock the door.

He was no sooner gone than Thunder turned his grey eyes on Nuwa, and burst into tears. 'Please, oh please, oh please, please, please!' he sobbed. 'Let me out or I'll die!'

Nuwa turned to face the wall, so as not to see him, and shook her head.

'Oh please, pretty-pity-please! Have mercy!' begged Thunder. 'How would you like it if a man with a cage trapped *your* father, and cooked him with herbs and spices and ate him for dinner?'

Nuwa bit her lip and put her arms over her head, trying not to listen.

'Well, all right, little one, I understand. Won't you just give me a drop to drink? Is that too much to ask?'

Nuwa thought this was the least she could do for the

poor beast in the cage. She ran at once and got a cup of water. Telling Thunder to go right to the other end of the cage, she put it through the bars.

The water was gone in one slurp, and Thunder's eyes turned an interesting blue. Then, to Nuwa's horror, the whole of him began to change – to swell – to grow, bigger and bigger, until he filled the cage like a dog in a cat-basket. He bulged through the bars, bent them, burst them like a whale bursting a string bag. Pieces of metal flew in every direction, some embedding themselves in the house wall, while Thunder funnelled into the sky in a single dark column of cloud. As he passed the tree-tops, he picked a gourd from the branches and threw it down to Nuwa, calling, '*One kindness deserves another!*'

Seeing the commotion in the distance as he rode home, Smith dug in his heels and came back at the gallop. The awful truth was all too plain: his captive gone, his hopes of dinner, too. And over his house hung Retribution: enough rain to flood not only his home, his garden, his country, but the wide world!

So Smith began work. 'I'll deal with you later!' he snarled at his two terrified little children.

The wreck of his cage made the keel, and his iron barn made the walls. He was the best blacksmith for miles around and he worked fast, but long before he finished, the rain had begun to fall. First drizzle, then sprinkling rain, then a downpour, then hail and sleet and snow all mixed together tumbled out of the sky to the noise of a thousand kettledrums, as Thunder wrought his revenge.

But when Smith's iron ship was finished, the last rivet hammered home, no one but he went on board. 'What do I need with two such worthless children?' he shouted down from the quarterdeck. 'Sink or swim, but don't look to me for any help: you brought this on us, and now you can pay!'

The floodwater soon came up to Nuwa's waist. It set the

iron ship afloat to grate and bump about. Swiftly, Nuwa picked up a knife and cut a hole in the gourd, and she and her brother climbed inside.

The Flood rolled over the Earth in swirls and eddies, joining lake to lake, river to river. Soon all the houses in the world disappeared from sight – all the trees, all the hills, all the mountains. Still Thunder poured down rain on to the Earth. People riding out the Flood in boats and bath-tubs and basins called out to God to help them, but God was sound asleep, lulled by the hush-shushing of the falling rain. Their puny voices could not rouse Him.

Not until the floodwater reached Heaven itself did He stir.

Bang bang bang. 'Wake up, won't you?' he heard. *Bang clang bang* 'Wake up, you old fool! What does it take to get your attention?' It was foul-tempered Smith, beating on the floor of Heaven from underneath with his iron fork, CLANG BANG CLANG.

Startled and bleary, God looked around him. He saw the Earth and sky full to the brim with floodwater, and the pavings of Heaven starting to lift. 'Waters, be gone!' He commanded.

And the Flood was gone.

It did not drain away, soak in, evaporate in the hot sun. No. It just went. One moment it was there, then, with a clap of God's hands, it was gone. One thousand miles deep and as wide as the world, it just disappeared, leaving a mighty long way down for those who had been floating around on its surface.

The iron ship plummeted down, like a bell falling from a cathedral steeple one thousand miles high. It landed with a single dull CLANG.

But the gourd, of course, fell as any gourd falls from trees: gently, with a spongy PLOP, into a puddle of mud. And Nuwa and her little brother climbed out unharmed.

Thunder saw to that.

'One kindness deserves another,' growled the dark and distant clouds. So Nuwa and her brother planted the seeds from inside the gourd, and from those grew the first plants of the new Earth, and Nuwa and her brother lived all alone beneath their shade, while the world began anew.

A Prickly Situation

BEAVER had been beavering away all summer. Busy, busy, busy. His dam was built, he had plenty of food for the winter. 'My larder is full,' he said, congratulating himself as he pushed an arrowhead ripple across the pool with his nose. 'Not like hers,' he thought as he saw Porcupine sitting idly on the bank. She was still sitting there later in the day. '*My* larder is full,' Beaver thought gleefully as he pushed another ripple back across the pool, swimming homeward.

His larder was empty.

Beaver caught up with Porcupine on a forest path, pushing a large barrow full of food. 'You stole my food, you bone-idle bunch of no-good knitting needles!'

'Me? Never. I'm a porcupine. Porcupines don't steal,' replied Porcupine.

Beaver took a look into the barrow. The food was familiar. Beaver-type food. So he went to take a large bite out of Porcupine's nose.

At the last moment, Porcupine tucked in her nose and fanned out her spines. It was like biting on a pincushion. Beaver jumped backwards, yelping and whimpering, with a noseful of spines, while Porcupine rattled away, swinging her rump about like a mace.

When the Beaver People saw the state of Beaver's nose, they felt the smart as though it were their own. 'This is war!' they declared. 'That porcupine has eaten her last dinner!'

An army as huge and plush as a bearskin lay siege to Porcupine's house, and when she would not come out, knocked it down and dragged her away. This time they used ropes. There wasn't a thing Porcupine could do to save herself. Over leaves and stones, over beach and out to sea they towed the thief, marooning her on an island seven miles offshore. Not husband, child, friend or neighbour could find hide or spine of her, though they searched and searched.

Dismayed and discomforted, Porcupine listened to the rhythmic splash of her enemies' oars as they rowed away and left her. Then shaking herself, with a noise like spillikins, she looked around the island. No berry bushes, no farm crops, no shops. There was not even so much as a tree to chew the bark off, not a string of seaweed washed up on the beach. 'They mean me to starve!' said Porcupine, choking back a sob. 'Well, I shan't give them the satisfaction! I'll drown myself in the sea! . . . in a minute or two.' Being an idle creature, Porcupine sat down for a rest.

A gentle breeze was blowing across the island, and in it the first bitter seeds of winter. Also a voice. At least, it *sounded* like a voice in Porcupine's ear, saying, '*Call the North Wind, your kin! Call on the North Wind!*'

Porcupine was not of a mystical turn of mind. She had no faith in chants or spells. So she paid no heed – only hunched and slumped her way around and around her barren prison until, in her hunger, she could count her ribs as easily as her spines. Her eyesight was smeary and her ears rang. They rang with that same voice: '*Summon the North Wind, your kin! Summon up the Wind!*'

Porcupine had nothing to lose, and there was no one close by to snigger, so she lifted up her nose and sang the chant:

'Come you North Wind, full of winter!
Come you North Wind, full of snow!
Come you steel-grey, glass-sharp splinter
in the sky's eye, North Wind BLOW!'

Spiny with hail and sleet, rattling and bristling with icicles, the North Wind heard, and came howling down from the Arctic. There were no trees to groan or bend, no beasts but Porcupine to shiver in the icy blast. But the sand swirled in eddies across the beach, and the sea slopped gelatinous against the shore.

Yes, the sea gelled and stood still. Its waves were trapped under a crust of ice as, gradually, the sea froze solid as far as the horizon. Sadly, poor Porcupine was too feeble to move, too weakened by hunger to crawl out on to that magic ice and escape!

Porcupine's relations, searching the shoreline, were amazed at the sight of the sea freezing over. They set off at once across its furrowing, fretful surface, to search all the islands offshore. Last of all, they came to a knoll so small and bare they would never even have spotted it but for the dark spiny shape rolled up in a ball on the sand. Porcupine!

She had to be carried home and fed cabbage broth through a quill straw. The sight of her was so piteous that her family quite forgot the crime which had been her undoing. 'This is war!' they declared. 'That beaver must pay!'

An army as prickly and numberless as the conker cases under a chestnut tree stormed Beaver's lodge. And though his huge dam proved as impenetrable as a castle wall, the porcupines did manage to take one prisoner. Beaver himself was captured and dragged away, over mud, over stones and through the forest.

'You marooned Porcupine and left her to starve! Now we'll maroon you, Rug-tail!' They dragged him over treetops and up the trunk of the tree. Like a lynch-mob they swung him from one branch up to the next, until he burst headfirst out of the very crown of the tree. 'Bet you didn't know porcupines could climb trees, did you? Eh? Eh, Bugsbeaver? Now see how you like a taste of your own medicine!' And so saying they left him, marooned him, abandoned him at the top of the tallest tree in the forest.

Around him a sea of trees waved in late autumnal tides of orange and gold. Beaver shook the leaves out of his fur and listened to the rattle of a dozen porcupines shinnying down the tree. Then he hummed a small tune to himself – not a magical chant or a mystical incantation – just a tune.

As he hummed, he began to gnaw. Gnaw, gnaw, gnaw. Beaver liked to keep busy. Busy, busy, busy. By next morning, he had gnawed his way through the entire tree, top to bottom. Then he trotted home to his pool, his dam and his lodge under the dam, to spend a peaceful winter relaxing with his family.

How the Fairies Became

A EUROPEAN LEGEND

BEFORE there was an earth to walk on or human feet to walk it, God parted Light from Dark. Pushing the darkness downwards, He lived above, in the Realms of Light, beside a glass sea. The darkness settled into a bottomless tarry lake, while the upper light crystallized into spires and domes surrounded by walls of cloud. Flitting about that heavenly citadel, like starlings at dusk, were the angels, doing whatever God asked.

That was the time of perfect happiness, so peaceful that God was free to begin His next creation: Earth. Once begun, it took up all His time – parting sea from land, colouring the animals . . . While He was away, rebellion stirred among the angels. Returning one day from creating the great fishes, God found His cherubim and seraphim brawling in the streets of Paradise. They talked of taking over from God and turning Him out of Heaven. They had even crowned a leader to take His place: an angel calling himself Lucifer, the Carrier of Light. That was the start of the Heavenly Wars, when comets were hurled like sling-shot and the skies rained meteors – God's men against Lucifer's.

Some, though, did not take sides. Whether they were cowards, or just wanted to be sure of siding with the winners, these "undecided" angels kept to the hidey-holes of Heaven, biding their time. In their smallness of spirit, they actually shrank, and their wings became transparent.

God won out, of course. Lucifer and all his troops were

defeated and toppled out of Heaven. They hurtled down into the tarry pool and the bottomless region of dark. The cloud walls were mended, and everything was the same as before in the marvellous Realms of Light.

Except for the Undecided.

They scurried to sit at God's feet. They sang His praises loudly. But at once He held up a hand to silence them.

'You cannot stay,' he said, and their transparent wings wilted. 'You would not help me when I needed you, and he who is not with me is against me. I shall not throw you into the tarry lake, but you must go and live in this new place I have made – on Earth. Live in the hills and under the ground; live among the tree roots and long grass. From today you shall be called fairies and pixies, brownies and sprites – not angels; not ever angels.'

'Do you hate us so much, then, Master?' said the tallest of the Undecided.

'I neither hate nor love you,' said God, 'because you neither loved nor hated me.'

The Undecided who flew down that day from Paradise to Earth were as plentiful as the dragonflies and thistledown: the people who lived there caught sight of fairies every day. But somehow, there have come to be fewer over the years. Perhaps their magic wore out and they became mortal and died. Or perhaps they shrank to a size human eyes cannot see.

Some people say that God, in His Kindness, forgave them one by one, and let them go home to Heaven, and that there their magic was put to grander use, building the Universe and hanging up the stars. But we shall not find out the truth yet awhile. Not in this life.

The Gods Down Tools

A SUMERIAN MYTH

'ENOUGH!' said Enki, throwing down his spade. 'For a thousand years we've dug out rivers and piled up hills. There has to be more to life than this!'

Around him, the other gods nodded and muttered. Spade after pick dropped to the ground. 'Let Enlil do it himself!'

It was a surly rabble of weary immortals which picketed the home of Enlil, Lord of the Winds. 'What's the matter?' he asked, when he came to the door. 'Why have you stopped working? You still have the River Tigris to dig! We must have that meander by Monday!'

'We're sick of digging,' said the gods. 'You've worn us out, Enlil. We're all agreed: no more digging.'

To their astonishment, Enlil burst into tears. 'I'm sorry! I never realized. I was a fool! I resign as world-planner! I do, I resign!'

The strikers shuffled their feet, embarrassed and a little shamefaced. The Lord of the Winds was a sensitive, passionate soul; they had not meant to hurt his feelings.

We-e coughed awkwardly. 'Suppose – just suppose,' he said, 'that we created some kind of creature to do the work for us?'

And thus humankind was invented – Nintur made them out of earth and blood – to finish digging the river and planting the fields.

They did very well, worked as industriously as the ants, *and* worshipped the gods as well, which gave the gods a warm and happy feeling they had not felt before. Nintur did not need to make thousands: they reproduced themselves. And when they were worn out and could not work any more, they died. Cities grew up, like ant hills, with homes and shops, bath houses and meeting halls. Carts trundled from place to place, and street sellers shouted all day long:

'Buy your fish! Fresh fish today!'

'Lots of lovely lemons!'

'Cage-birds, songbirds, going cheap!'

'WHAT IS THAT DIN?' demanded Enlil one day.

'It's the People,' Enki replied. 'Busy little things, aren't they?'

Enlil groaned and covered his ears. 'The noise! The racket!'

Now Enki had grown rather fond of humankind, and the noise did not much trouble him – except perhaps women who sang off-key and crying babies at night. 'Each separate one doesn't make much noise. It's just that there are so many these days.'

'Then *thin them out*!' hissed Enlil, his nerves frayed from lack of sleep. 'Send Plague to kill them, one in three.'

Regretfully, Enki summoned Plague and told her. But then he hurried ahead to the cities of Sumer, and warned the little workers.

When Plague arrived, everywhere was silent. The cart-wheels were muffled with cloth, the babies were all feeding, women passed by their neighbours without a word, and street sellers mimed on the street corners. What is more, delicious offerings were burning on every altar. Plague had not the heart to slaughter one in three, not even one in ten. Not one, in fact.

Enlil did not insist. The cities were silent. He was able to sleep at night and snooze in the afternoon. And he needed workers to build the Zagros Mountains.

For a thousand years, all went as well as it can in the best of all possible worlds. Parents told their children to be quiet, but the children forgot to tell their children. The noise gradually increased. Husbands nagged their wives, children squabbled over toys, women insisted on singing, in and out of key.

'Where can a god go to have some peace and quiet, with this chatter-chatter-chatter?' Enlil complained. 'Let the rivers dry up, let the lakes turn to salt. Perhaps when they are dead of thirst, these human beings will be silent!'

Enki hurried down to the cities of Sumer and warned them: unless they quieten their noise, a fearful drought would kill whole families, neighbourhoods, towns! The priests rushed to the temples of An, the water god, and heaped them with gifts. The men held their fingers to their lips, babies sucked their thumbs, and the din once more fell silent. An had not the heart to take their water, and Enlil had gone back to sleep.

For a thousand years all went as well as it can in the best of all possible worlds. Parents told their children to be quiet, and their children told theirs. But then someone said the story of the drought had never happened. A woman argued with him, and people took sides. Tempers flared, punches were thrown, and the fight that followed made more noise than all the street-traders in Sumer.

Enlil closed his windows. Enlil closed his doors. But still he could hear the din of the cities of Sumer. 'I WILL NOT HAVE THIS NOISE!' he bellowed. 'If they must open their mouths to shout and jabber, let them have no food to put in them, and let them starve and die, but GIVE ME SOME PEACE!'

The famine began instantly; there was no time for Enki to warn anybody. Crops withered, trees cankered, the berries were eaten by birds. The People grew thin as sticks, and had nothing but water to give their children. They called on Enki to save them.

But how to help? Enki paced the banks of the Tigris, stalked the fruitless woods, thinking. Then with a cry of inspiration, he ran to the river and threw in a handful of magic.

Thirty thousand fish tumbled down the river – a coppery shoal of bream and carp overspilling the banks and leaping clear of the waves. There were so many that the People had only to reach out a hand to grasp a fin, a tail, a fishy feast. After that, their mouths were too crammed to talk. Also, fishing is a quiet pursuit, so that Enlil, though angry, let the famine end. 'Next time . . .' he muttered. 'Next time . . .'

For a thousand years, all went as well as it can in the best of all possible worlds. Parents told their children to hush, and their children told their grandchildren. But babies will cry, and neighbours will quarrel. A man must sell his wares. People laugh at jokes, and children cry when they fall over.

Enlil tried to sleep on one ear, then he tried to sleep on the other. But the noise of the cities of Sumer was howling pandemonium in his head.

'AWAY WITH THE LOT OF THEM!' he thundered. 'Let the Earth know silence again. Drown every mortal!'

With the winds in his keeping, he piled up the waves of the sea and thrust rain into the rivers till they burst their banks. He plugged up the tunnels under the earth and gathered the rainclouds like a flock of sheep. This time Enki could see no way to save the People: no possible way . . . unless he were to save just one . . .

'Beware! Beware, Atrahasis!' he whispered to the best of his mortal friends. 'The Lord of the Winds is sending a flood! Build a boat – a big boat – and take your family aboard, along with two of every kind of animal . . .'

Perhaps you have heard the story, or some version of it.

For seven days and seven nights water rolled down the rivers and cascaded out of the sky, drowning all the crying and laughing, shouting and music, traffic and building and singing. The last sounds to trouble Enlil came from swimmers crying for help to the gods, and rooks shrieking in the drowning trees. Then everything was silent.

The gods looked down in horror at the world they had dug and shaped and peopled. They saw their altars and the flowers from their altars float by on the Flood. All this for the sake of peace and quiet?

As the Flood soaked away, Atrahasis' boat ran aground on a mountain top, and he set loose the animals. They ploughed, muddy-legged, through the ruined crops and fallen buildings, the wreckage of the Flood.

'We must offer thanks to the gods that we were saved,' was the first thing Atrahasis said.

When Enlil woke from his peaceful sleep, he looked down at the empty earth and saw . . . Atrahasis.

'Kill him!' he cried, bursting into tears. 'Kill him, or he'll breed! I can see it now! People marrying, people multiplying! Soon it will be as bad as ever! Kill Atrahasis!'

He gave the order, but none of the other gods moved.

'Kill him!' screamed Enlil, making more noise than anyone.

'I'm hungry,' said Enki.

'The fields need tending,' said Nanna. 'Who will do it, if not Atrahasis and the sons and daughters of Atrahasis?'

'There's a lot of *mending* to be done,' said An, pointedly.

'Must we do it all ourselves?' said We-e.

'Must we do everything?' they asked. And one by one, Enki led the gods away, leaving Enlil amid the silence of solitude.

They say Atrahasis was a soft-spoken man, and that he raised his children to speak softly, too. Even with all the gods but one on his side, Atrahasis knew better than to take chances.

Balder and the Mistletoe

A NORSE MYTH

BALDER woke screaming from a terrible nightmare, and laid his hand against his chest. 'Weep!' he cried. His wife, waking beside him, tried to calm him. 'Think, my love! What can possibly harm you? Nothing can pierce your golden skin. Nothing can bruise your soft flesh. And you've no enemies! Everyone loves you as much as I do. Shsh now. There's nothing to be afraid of.' But she could not rid his eyes of terror or the stain of that dreadful dream.

Freya, Queen of the gods, heard her son cry out. It was not for the first time he had dreamed of danger, of dying, and she was worried.

'Who would want to harm our son?' snorted Odin, Balder's father and the King of all gods. 'He's the darling of the world!'

But Freya, like her dream-plagued son, could not rest easy. She decided to exact a promise from every living thing; never to harm her son.

She asked the birds, including the ravenous ravens, the scavenging vultures and the soaring eagles. They all swore never to hurt Balder.

She asked the wild beasts and the tame; the savage lion, the strangling snake and all the venomous hairy spiders. They swore never to hurt Balder.

She asked the flies and the flowers, the fish and the whales, the anemones and the octopuses. and they all swore never to harm a hair of Balder's handsome head.

She asked the thorn bushes and the heather, the smallest herb and the highest oak tree never to harm her beloved son. But she did not see, clinging to the oak like a lantern of luminous green, the gentle mistletoe which grows among the oak leaves, but which is neither leaf nor seed nor berry nor twig of the tree itself.

'All is well, son. You can sleep sound tonight,' she told Prince Balder.

But in the sunny woods, hidden between the tall timber and taller sunbeams, Loki the Trouble-Maker grinned to himself. A piece of mischief had occurred to him, the kind of work for which only he, Loki the Trickster, Loki the Outsider, Loki the Anarchist was framed. He saw how Freya had missed the mistletoe. She had not asked Loki for his promise, either.

Loki bore Balder no hatred, but, for Loki, a peaceful world was as loathsome as dead calm to a sailor. He needed a storm to fill his sails.

'Is it true what they say, Balder?' said Loki. 'That nothing can harm you?'

'Nothing,' said Balder, all his good humour restored. 'Try me! Hit me! Punch me! Go on!' and he offered the flat, steely muscles of his stomach for Loki to punch.

Loki saw misgiving flash through Queen Freya's eyes; she knew how unpredictable Loki could be. But Loki only shrugged his shoulders and shook his head. 'Couldn't possibly. You know me. Wouldn't harm a fly.'

Even so, thanks to Loki's question, all the other gods were soon cheerfully heaving rocks and spears and trees and goats and cats and clouds and all manner of everything at the magnificent figure of Prince Balder – just to test the magic. And nothing so much as grazed his golden skin.

Even Balder's blind brother, Hodir, was easily caught up in the game. Loki had only to slip a loaf, a fir-cone, a pigeon in between Hodir's fingers and he joined in the throwing. After that, Loki had only to slip a stem of mistletoe into Hodir's hand . . . The tender white berries trickled to the ground between Hodir's fingers.

No kiss came with this mistletoe, no loving kindness. It flew, stuck fast, and pierced Balder's chest, sharp and deep as any needle. Balder looked down with an expression of faint surprise on his lovely face. Then he dropped like the oak tree on which the mistletoe had once grown, while the other gods gasped and cried out, and blind Hodir asked, 'What? What's happened? What's wrong?'

Queen Freya held her hair in both hands and screamed a scream which shivered the glass windows of the sky. 'NO!' she cried. 'NO! NO! He shan't die! My son shan't die!'

Hermodir, younger brother of Balder and Hodir, ran to King Odin. 'Lend me your horse, Father! If I ride fast enough, maybe I can stop him – snatch back his soul before it reaches Helheim!'

Odin did not hesitate. He tossed the reins of Sleipnir, his eight-legged horse, into the hands of his youngest son. 'Tell Queen Hel she must wait for my son. Tell her we cannot spare him yet to her Kingdom of the Dead!'

And so, while the gods held their breaths, and the forests of the world quivered with shock, Hermodir spurred on Spleipnir to gallop as the beast had never galloped before.

Faster than thought, Sleipnir's eight hooves covered the miles. For a whole day Hermodir rode, and at every moment he expected to see the soul of Balder flying ahead of him towards the gates of the Underworld.

Faster than light, Sleipnir's eight hooves sped down deep valleys and ravines. For nine whole days Hermodir rode until at last he came to a golden bridge spanning a rushing river of ink-black water, and he heard, along the planks of the bridge, the footsteps of his dead brother still echoing. He knew he was entering the Kingdom of Helheim, territory of Queen Hel, Goddess of Death, but his courage never wavered. Into Helheim, into the hall of Hel herself, rode Hermodir, just as she reached out to clasp Balder's ghostly hand.

'WAIT!'

Hermodir rode between them. Sleipnir snorted and sweated and steamed, stamping his eight feet.

'Wait, Goddess of Death, and listen! The world cannot bear to part with Balder! Hodir will never forgive himself! The great god Odin's heart will break, and Queen Freya may flood the earth with her tears! Let him go! Let his soul go back to his body! Spare him just this once to his mother and father and brothers and friends! Have pity, Queen Hel!'

Hel stroked the neck of Spleipnir, so that the horse's sweat turned to ice and fell to the ground like gravel. 'If all the creatures of the earth are ready to shed a tear for Balder, and if I may have all those tears to slake my thirst, you may have back your brother. I would not grant as much to any other man. Tell Freya this.'

So for nine days, Hermodir rode back – across the golden bridge, up valleys and ravines, to the sunlit world, and there he returned to the forest clearing where Balder's dead body still lay, a sprig of mistletoe piercing his chest. Hermodir proclaimed the price of Balder's life.

'Then he's free!' cried Freya, laughing through her tears. 'Every creature in Creation is *already* weeping for my boy!'

It was true. It was almost true. It was true of all but one. For when Freya came face-to-face with Loki, she saw no tear in his swirling eyes.

'Weep, Loki!' she commanded. 'You more than anyone should be sorry! You put the mistletoe into Hodir's hand!'

But Loki would not weep. 'I am framed to bring disorder where there is peace, storm where there is calm.'

'Weep, Loki!' raged the Queen.

But Loki would not weep. 'I was framed to trick the simple and teach the innocent not to be so trusting.'

'Weep, Loki, I beg you!' pleaded the Queen, falling to her knees.

But Loki would not weep. 'What's done is done, and I did it. Nor shall I shed one tear of regret. Let Hel hold what she has!' And he laughed in Freya's face, laughed and glared, dry-eyed.

'Launch a great ship,' said Odin, straightening his ancient back. 'A warship. Lay Balder's body on the deck. His soul will not be returning from the Underworld. Thanks to Loki, my son belongs to Queen Hel now, and is lost to us everlastingly.'

But as that ship sailed out to sea – as torches were thrown into Balder's funeral barge, and its sails billowed into rags and flags of scarlet fire – Odin took hold of Loki the Trouble-Maker and lashed him in chains, buried him in the earth, and set the poison of a giant serpent to drip, drip, drip everlastingly on to the god's face.

No death came to the rescue of Loki-the-Unquiet, Loki-the-Trickster. No pity came from any creature in the wide world, except his wife, whose tears, falling in his face, diluted the poison. Now, whenever the Mischief-Maker writhes in agony under the drops of poison, the whole Earth shakes and quakes with seismic horror.

Still Loki does not weep – not for Balder, and not for himself. For what he did, he was framed to do. It was in his nature to do it, just as it is in the nature of living things to die.

About the Stories

All these stories have been passed down from generation to generation by word of mouth and changed a little by each successive storyteller, growing and altering to suit the listener. I have retold them – sometimes from the briefest passing reference in dusty old volumes – to please you, the reader. In doing so, I have made sometimes small, sometimes large changes, but have tried to preserve an inkling of the pleasure each story gave to its original audience.

G McC.

The Silver-Miners
Bolivians enjoy an almost personal relationship with the landscape that surrounds them. I am indebted to M. Rigoberto Paredes and his book *Mitos, Supersticiones y Supervivencias Populares de Bolivia* for the contents of this story.

The Men in the Moon
The Chaga people of Kenya display, in this story, a unique concept of the Moon being attached to the Earth by a causeway.

Dream Journey
The dangers, frustrations and responsibilities of leadership are a large aspect of this Maori story about an exceptionally enlightened chief.

Roland and the Horn Olivant
In AD 778, Basque warriors annihilated the rearguard of Charlemagne's retreating army. As the story was retold, Saracens were substituted for the Basques. The epic poem, *Chanson de Roland*, recounting Roland's heroic last stand, was written in the early twelfth century.

A QUESTION OF LIFE AND DEATH
During the fourth century BC, The Boeotian city of Thebes was briefly the leading power-base within the Greek Empire. Sophocles wrote a play about Oedipus, a legendary king of Thebes – a sorry tale from start to finish, but for his defeat of the Sphinx.

THE HARP OF DAGDA
The Dagda, or Daghdha, was the Irish 'good god' or 'great father'. 'The Mighty One of Great Knowledge'. He could kill and restore life with his giant club, and had control over harvests and the weather. His worship was prevalent around 200 BC.

A NEST AND A WEB
In AD 622, Muhammad moved from Mecca to Medina, on a journey now called the Hejira or migration. It marks year one of the Muslim calendar. This is a story told about that journey.

ASH
This is a shortened retelling of the life and feats of strength of Duktuthl, or 'Dirty Skin', told by the Tlingit tribe inhabiting the north-west coast of North America and Canada.

THE TOWER OF BABEL
The plain where the tower was said to have been built is the Tigris-Euphrates basin where Mesopotamian civilizations erected ziggurat temples as gateways to Heaven. It was originally told, not as a warning against pride and ambition, but simply to explain the origin of languages.

SAINT CHRISTOPHER
'Thou hast borne all the world upon thee, and its sins likewise,' says the child to Christopher in an antique English telling of the traditional European tale. Dr Brewer in *Myth and Legend* writes, 'This is an allegory: Christopher means Christbearer; the child was Christ, and the river was the river of death.'

GOD MOVES AWAY
Togo is one of the smallest countries in Africa, sandwiched between Ghana and Benin, in the west. Its chief crop is maize, so it is no

surprise that the pounding of maize with pestle and mortar features in its myths.

WILHELM TELL
It has never been possible to track down a real-life figure on whom Wilhelm Tell might be based. He seems to be a fifteenth-century invention, exactly mirroring the Norse *Saga of Thidrek* in which Egil the Archer shoots an apple off his son's head.

A HEART OF STONE
The Greek myth of Pygmalion, as told in the Latin poet Ovid's *Metamorphoses,* was the basis for George Bernard Shaw's modern comedy, *Pygmalion*, and thus for the musical *My Fair Lady*. Aphrodite was the Greek goddess of love: Ovid used the name of Venus, her Roman equivalent.

BABUSHKA
'Babuskha' simply means 'grandmother' in Russian, and is used of any old peasant lady. She is the Russian equivalent of Saint Nicholas, her poignant story explaining the tradition of giving presents to children at Christmas.

THE PIG GOES COURTING
Kamapua'a's name means 'hog child', and his hilarious mythology largely explains features of Hawaiian geology and natural phenomena. He is impulsive and unpredictable – a good friend to have around, but something of a liability, too.

CAN KRISHNA DIE?
Though Krishna's name means 'the black one', he is usually depicted as having a blue face of ineffable beauty. He features in the ancient Hindu text the *Bhagavad-Gita* as an avatar (or incarnation) of the god Vishnu.

THE LIGHTHOUSE ON THE LAKE
The hurricanes which frequently rage across Japan's Lake Biwa in August are called Hira hurricanes, because they blow from the Hira mountain range. The myth of the lighthouse-keeper is an attempt to explain this seasonal cataclysm.

KING ARTHUR GIVES BACK HIS SWORD
The ninth-century *Historia Britonum* mentions a warlord called Arthur leading the Saxons in twelve battles culminating in a triumphant victory in about 500 BC. The Arthurian tradition has little to do with him, however, and grew up during the Age of Chivalry, feeding off Celtic legend and Christian allegory.

A BLOODTHIRSTY TALE
Hathor, benign and gentle goddess of Egyptian mythology, was also the fearful Sekhmet – Powerful One. On her feast day, the preparation of strong drink was entrusted to girls instead of men, and toasts drunk to the goddess. She thus became goddess of wine.

RIP VAN WINKLE
American writer Washington Irving gave him a name in his *The Sketch Book of Geoffrey Crayon, Gent.* But Rip Van Winkle existed long before that, in legend and rumour, among the Catskill Mountains.

THE RAVEN AND THE MOON
There are many variants of this story. Its original function was to explain why the moon waxes and wanes. Raven is the Inuit animal of creation, responsible for making the world and unearthing the sun from the ground.

SIR PATRICK SPENS
In AD 1266 Norway renounced claims on the Hebrides in return for a marriage between Prince Eric of Norway and Princess Margaret of Scotland. In 1281 the Princess embarked for Norway and her wedding. On the return trip, a terrible storm sank the ship which had carried her.

THE SALTCELLAR
The many variants of this worldwide myth have littered the sea bed with mills and cellars, all churning out salt. This version is Scandinavian. Though it may seem odd for the pirates to rate salt a precious cargo, it was once a vital and priceless food preservative.

THE BRONZE CAULDRON
In sixth-century Wales there lived a gifted poet named Taliesin. But

even if he were the dim and distant origin of this legendary figure, the stories told about 'bright brow' contain truly ancient and recurring elements of myth: shape-changing, prophecy, the 'thumb of knowledge' (as it is in Ireland). Legendary Taliesin even sailed with King Arthur to Otherworld to recover British treasures stolen by the forces of evil.

THE BATTLE OF THE DRUMS
The Mandan tribe of native North Americans live on the plains, dependent on the buffalo herds for food and shelter. Lone Man is their 'founding father' and protector, this story the origin of their ritual chants, dance and drumming.

CUPID AND PSYCHE
Here is a remarkable ancestor of a fairy tale now popular the world over. *East o' the Sun, West o' the Moon* is easily recognizable in this Roman myth. It may have been first set down in writing by Apuleius, in the second century AD, in his book *The Golden Ass*. Since Psyche means 'soul' and Cupid represents physical love, the story is also about the two elements at work in true love.

DOCTOR FAUST
Georgius Sabellious lived in sixteenth-century Germany: a doctor, fortune-teller, astrologer and magician. He roused the anger of the Church, but had several rich and influential clients. After his death, the rumours about him were wild and inventive. 'Faustus Junior' (as he called himself) became the subject of fairground puppet shows.

ALONE
The Native Americans of the North-West Pacific coast tell this story of a time before the region was populated. It is extraordinary not only for its wistful melancholy, but also for the picture of a primeval world devoid of men, heroic or otherwise.

THE GOLDEN VANITY
This story is usually sung as a ballad. There are many versions, the oldest of which names the treacherous Captain as Sir Walter Raleigh, no less, and the ship as his vessel *Sweet Trinity*.

The Founding of London

The founding of London is one small incident in the thirteenth-century saga of Ragnar Lodbrok (or Ragnar Leather-Trousers). In it England figures simply as one overseas colony among all the others which the Danesmen conquered.

The Monster with Emerald Teeth

Most knowledge of the Mayan culture of Central America comes from the *Popul Vub* (Collection of Written Leaves). Lost in the seventeenth century, it turned up after two hundred years in Guatemala, and contains stories collated by the Mayans themselves before they, like the giants, disappeared from the earth.

The Golem

The 'historical' Golem of Prague in Czechoslovakia probably gave rise to a latter, better-known fiction – *Frankenstein*. Its brief life was the subject of a novel by Gustav Meyrink in 1916, written three hundred years after the supposedly true events.

Mummy's Baby

This story is told by the Eskimos of West Greenland. Though only a guess, it seems fairly plain that Kakuarshuk's subterranean journey is a mystical depiction of labour and childbirth itself.

Dear Dog

The Japanese tell countless variations of this story, the good kami of an animal or person passing into other living things, bringing help to the deserving, punishment to the wicked. Plants in particular are seen as selflessly devoted to those who treat them tenderly, and it is a heinous crime indeed to cut down a beautiful tree.

Monkey Do: The Story of Hanuman

Hanuman, son of the Hindu wind god, is a divine being. For helping Rama, he is rewarded with eternal youth. The exploits of the two are set down in the seven-volume *Ramayana,* one of the great epic works of Sanskrit literature, composed by the poet Valmiki in 500 BC. Even to read the *Ramayana* is an act so holy as to absolve the reader of sin. When Hanuman's fame spread to China, he became hugely popular there, too, and the subject of new adventures.

A BOUQUET OF FLOWERS
The aboriginal peoples of Australia tell various stories of Baiame, the 'Father Spirit', who lived on Earth as a man for a short time so as to rest after completing Tya (the world). He promised to return to visit them, now and then, in human form.

THE CURIOUS HONEYBIRD
This Bantu version of Pandora's Box also incorporates the belief of one section of Bantu – the Kaonde – surrounding Leza's withdrawal from his creation. This apparent aloofness of the creator, taking offence after a period of initial tenderness, recurs time and time again throughout Africa.

THE SKY-BLUE STORYBOX
The Ashanti tribe of Ghana were once rich and powerful masters of the 'Gold Coast'. The first outsiders to hear their tales of Anansi the Spider Man and Nyame the Sky God were Portuguese merchant-sailors. But they cared more for the local currency – gold dust – and the strong slaves to be had, than for the wealth of vivid stories.

A QUESTION OF ARITHMAGIC
Olaf Tryggvason ruled Norway from AD 995 to 1000. A series of stories recount his various confrontations with heathen gods and malevolent trolls, all of which give the impression that the Old Magic is more potent than the new (Christianity), though the King does always win *in the end*.

THE ALCHEMIST
Two thousand years ago, alchemy – the magical chemistry of transmuting valueless substances into precious ones – intensely interested the Taoist priests of China. Whereas alchemists in Europe were usually seen as in league with the Devil, the Chinese ones were virtuous Immortals revisiting Earth.

WORKSHY RABBIT
The Hausa tribes of West Africa tell this particular fable of small outsmarting big. Wherever Rascal Rabbit pops up (as far apart as North America, Japan and Asia), his trickery and cunning are always admirable rather than reprehensible. Rabbit rarely meets with retribution.

CAT V. RAT
This story would have been told in scores of Congolese villages by the 'Alo Man' or story-teller, who travelled about spreading his repertoire of entertaining fables.

THE PIED PIPER
The German Pied Piper dates from 1298, when Hamelin's children were reputedly lured away by a magician and never seen again. The legend has been used to explain where isolated Germanic-speaking groups came from – the lost children of Hamelin re-emerging elsewhere from underground. Another theory is that the story masks the real-life tragedy of the Children's Crusade when whole populations of children did willingly leave their homes, incited by the Pope to fight a holy war. They never returned.

GULL-GIRL
This Chukchi myth from the bleak landscapes of Siberia is very like the European mermaid myths in which a fisherman takes a 'sulkie's' tailskin and hides it so that she cannot return to the sea. Torn between husband and natural instincts, the mermaid inevitably finds the tail and swims away, mourning the children she is forced to leave behind on dry land.

ARION AND THE DOLPHINS
Arion really was a poet at the court of the tyrant Periander – probably around 625 BC, though the legend of his rescue is pure poetic licence. In an older Greek myth, Dionysius, god of agriculture, is captured by pirates who leap overboard in terror when they realize who he is. He transforms them into the world's first dolphins.

THUNDER AND SMITH
Almost every culture has its own Flood myth – a cataclysm in prehistory when the world was cleansed by water and begun afresh. This Chinese Flood is brought about by the pride of a mortal who foolishly believes he can tame the elements. But it is unusual in that God escapes responsibility for the destruction: Thunder is blamed instead.

A PRICKLY SITUATION
In the original Haida myth, both Beaver and Porcupine are spirit

animals (though Porcupine's spines are no less substantial for that). The Haida are a Native North American people living both on the British Columbian mainland and the sprinkling of islands offshore: the Queen Charlotte Islands. And North American porcupines *can* climb trees!

How the Fairies Became
An apocryphal story dating from the time when the Christian Church was trying to absorb folkloric beliefs into an all-embracing faith. Thus a belief in fairies was no longer incompatible with being a good Christian.

The Gods Down Tools
Creator gods are not generally pictured as manual labourers, but the Sumerian gods of Babylonia are credited with creating mankind to take their place after the gods downed pick and shovel themselves, and went on strike.

Balder and the Mistletoe
Among the Scandinavian gods of Asgard, Balder was god of light. More than one myth accounts for his death – in one, Hodir is his rival in love and kills him in a fight – but one idea remains constant: Balder's death begins the Twilight of the Gods, the destruction of the halls of Asgard – Ragnarok, the Day of Doom. From the ruins of the Old World is born a new one in which Balder returns.